ERUPTION

Written by James M. Corkill.

Edition 1.

Chapter 1

NORTH AMERICA. SAN DIEGO, CALIFORNIA:

Marcus Hunter was standing on the dock beside his one-hundred-foot motorsailer named *Windancer*, ready to head out to a small harbor on the southern coast of Peru. He scratched the stubble of his beard as he looked down at his fourteen-year-old granddaughter, Geneva Hunter, who was ignoring him while texting. The last time he saw her, she was six years old and four feet tall, but now she was five foot nine and still growing.

He looked up and smiled when he saw his forty-three-year-old daughter, Doctor Olivia Hunter, strolling along the dock while pulling a large suitcase on wheels. Beside her was her eighteen-year-old daughter, Rickie Hunter, who was also pulling a suitcase.

Olivia stopped and gave Marcus a hug. "Hi, Dad. It's good to see you again."

"It's good to see you, too."

When everyone had their backs to her, Geneva looked up from her phone to study her long-lost relatives. She recognized her cousin from the funeral, but seemed shorter than she remembered. As Olivia turned and stared at her, she stopped breathing and quickly turned away, then began texting her girlfriend in Reno while trying to get rid of the knot in her stomach.

Rickie wondered what had caused Geneva's stunned reaction to seeing her aunt, then she turned to Marcus and wrapped her arms around his neck for a quick hug. "Hi, Grandpa. I'm looking forward to this new adventure."

Rickie stepped back and studied her cousin, who was ignoring her while still texting. They grew up in different sides of society, and she had not seen Geneva in eight years. She studied the tattoo of a three-headed snake on Geneva's right arm, not sure what to expect from the young girl from Reno, Nevada. All she knew was Geneva had spent more time on the streets than at home with her other grandparents. "Hey, Cuz. I doubt you remember me."

When Geneva ignored her and continued texting, Rickie turned to her grandfather. "How soon can we leave?"

"As soon as you and Geneva take in the mooring lines."

Marcus grabbed Rickie's suitcase, then he and Olivia went across the gangway up onto his ship and disappeared below deck. Rickie removed the spring line, coiling the rope over her arm and cinching it closed with a loop before tossing it onto the deck. When she noticed Geneva still texting, she moved in front of her, then folded her arms across her chest. "Are you going to help me?"

Geneva didn't look up. "I'm not a sailor, so I don't know what to do. I'm sure you can handle it."

Rickie snatched the phone from Geneva's hand and held it out over the water. "I'm glad you're offering to help me by releasing that stern line."

Geneva's hands clenched into fists at her sides as she glared at Rickie. "Give me my phone or I swear I'll kill you!"

Even though they were nearly the same height, Rickie was not intimidated and slid the phone into her back pocket. "Not yet. You need to earn the right to use it on our trip."

Geneva was surprised her intimidation expression wasn't working on her cousin, who she barely remembered. She caught movement in her peripheral vision, but continued glaring at Rickie. "Fine with me. I didn't want to go on this stupid boat trip in the first place. Give me my phone and I'm out of here."

When Marcus stepped out onto the main deck, he saw the girls down on the dock, staring at each other. "What's the holdup?"

Rickie continued locking stares with her cousin. "Nothing, Grandpa. We're just getting to know each other."

Geneva broke eye contact to look up at Marcus on the ship. "She said I don't have to go with you, so I'm going to get my stuff and go home."

Rickie pulled the phone from her pocket, smiling as she held it out to Geneva. "Don't forget your pacifier."

Geneva glared at Rickie as she snatched the phone from her hand, then slid it into her pocket as she stomped across the gangway onto the ship. She stopped at the top and looked at Rickie, who was still smiling at her, then she gave her the finger before disappearing below deck to pack her belongings.

Rickie looked up at Marcus. "I got this. Start the engines and let's get going before she gets her stuff."

Marcus grinned and hurried into the pilothouse, then started the engines driving the generators for the electric motor driven propellers. When Rickie ran up the gangway and began stowing it into a bracket, he engaged the thrusters to silently move the *Windancer* away from the dock. Once clear of the other ships, he rotated the thrusters to move the *Windancer* forward into the harbor.

***

Geneva shoved the last of her clothes into a large backpack, then shoved a fresh pack of cigarettes into her shirt pocket. She left her cabin and hurried up the stairs to the main deck, then froze in place when she realized they were in the middle of the harbor.

She tossed her backpack onto the deck, then stomped up the outside stairs into the pilothouse. She kept her clenched fists at her side as she glared at the back of Marcus, who was sitting in a captain's chair at the helm, and Rickie facing her from the chair next to him. "Take me back to the dock or I'll jump over the side and swim back!"

When Rickie smirked at her, Geneva moved over to the other chair next to Marcus, but didn't sit down. "Did you hear what I said?"

Marcus looked over at her. "I'm sorry, but I can't leave you alone on the mainland."

"I can take care of myself."

"I'm sure you can, but now you're my responsibility. This will be a good opportunity for all of us to get to know each other."

"By bobbing around on the water? No thanks. I'm leaving."

Rickie waited until Geneva was about to step outside. "Don't forget your pacifier doesn't like salt water."

Geneva stopped and spun around. "I'll put it in a baggie."

"If you look out the window, you'll see it's a long swim to shore."

Geneva glared at them until Olivia came up the inside stairs. She avoided looking at her aunt as she headed out of the pilothouse and down the steps onto the main deck.

Marcus smiled when his two girls were sitting in the captain's chairs on both sides of him as he continued out into open water. When he turned south and the traffic thinned out, he raised the automated sails and they bellowed full of wind. The speed quickly increased as he shut down the engines, and the only sound was the whisper of the wind through the open side windows.

He looked out the front window, where Geneva was lying on a recliner in the shade of the white mainsail. She was the only child of his son, Thomas, who had been an aviation mechanic in the United States Air Force. When he was killed in combat eight years ago, her mother became an alcoholic and died when she crashed her car six months later. Geneva was raised by her mother's elderly grandparents, who were living on social security in Reno. When he learned she was getting into trouble, he thought going on an adventure with her family would be good for her, but she refused to leave. He had filed for custody and won, then yesterday he had flown to Reno to get her, even though she fiercely protested leaving her friends.

Olivia reached into a small refrigerator and grabbed a bottle of beer, then handed it to her father. "It's great to be on the water again."

Marcus grinned as he took the bottle and swallowed some of the cool liquid. "I'm glad to see you getting away from the city for a while. All the stress you put on yourself worrying about your patients isn't good for your mental health."

"I can't help it. Even now, I worry about some of the worst cases. I'm hoping this trip will help me forget about them for a while."

"It usually does."

Olivia looked past Marcus to see Rickie. "Do either of you know why Geneva is avoiding me?"

Rickie shrugged her shoulders. "No, but I think she's mad at all of us."

Marcus knew better. "I'm the one she's mad at for dragging her away from her friends. You're both just collateral damage."

Rickie leaned back in her chair. "Once we stop at our first foreign port, I'll take her in to town and she'll get over it."

"Thanks. I think you'll be good for her."

"Not that I'm too worried, Grandpa, but what kind of trouble did she get into in Reno that was so bad?"

"According to the police report, a man had her arrested for pulling a knife on him in the park and demanding money. She claimed he tried to rape her, but there were no witnesses to either claim. The judge dismissed the charges against her for attempted robbery with a weapon, but did not charge the man with attempted rape. I realized she needed someone to understand what she's going through, and who better than my two girls?"

Rickie looked out through the front window and down onto the deck at her cousin. "We'll try."

Chapter 2

Day 1

6:43 PM. PASADENA CALIFORNIA. NASA JET PROPULSION LABORATORY.

The team of eighteen scientists and engineers had discovered a six-hundred-mile diameter asteroid was going to pass outside our solar system, but seven months ago, there was an unexplained change in its trajectory, which had set it on a collision course with Earth. Now everyone on the team was quietly holding their breaths while staring at the image on a large wall monitor. It was coming from their nuclear tipped rocket, which was about to hit the asteroid.

The image from the rocket vanished and everyone turned to the other monitor on the wall, which was showing a graphic image of the asteroid's path through our solar system. When the line slowly changed, cheers and applause erupted in the room, followed by smiles, hugs, and handshakes. Their hard work had succeeded and the asteroid would miss the Earth by four thousand miles.

A soft beeping came from the computer speaker, while the monitor showed two objects on separate trajectories. One was the large asteroid, then the picture zoomed in on what had initially changed its course. It was a three-quarter-mile-diameter chunk of solid rock, which was now on an intercept course with Earth. According to the timer, it would enter the atmosphere in two hours.

***

INTERNATIONAL SPACE STATION:

Rhonda Pryor, a thirty-year-old mechanical engineer from Utah, had been on the station for five months, continuing the upgrade to the solar charging system started by her predecessors. At the moment, she was studying data on the monitor, showing an update on the smaller asteroid's trajectory. On another monitor, the exterior camera had locked onto the approaching rock and was tracking its approach.

Vincent Cristallis, a fifty-three-year-old botanist from Latvia, was floating in the zero gravity while looking over Rhonda's shoulder at the screen. Slightly behind him were his three fellow scientists, each holding onto a handle to keep from drifting away. He reached out and grabbed the back of Rhonda's chair to pull him closer to her. "What is the status of the asteroid's trajectory?"

Rhonda had gotten a bad vibe the first time she had touched Vincent's hand, and now he was breathing on her neck. "Move back and I'll tell you."

She smirked at the others, who were grinning at Vincent's annoyed expression as he pushed back from her head. "Good enough. Estimated impact is the central United States near South Dakota, in two minutes. They predict it will probably leave a small crater in a farmer's frozen field, and won't have too big an effect on the surrounding areas."

John Saint Paul, a microbiologist, was not so sure. "They should have let us go home in case something goes wrong."

Stacy Anglia, the crew doctor, tried to hide her anxiety. "We should be grateful the big one isn't going to hit the Earth."

Camilla Mamba kissed the medallion on the silver chain around her neck. "I have a bad feeling about this."

***

WASHINGTON D.C. THE WHITE HOUSE OVAL OFFICE:

President Raymond Brill was with his Chief of Staff, Mark Grant, watching the broadcast of the approaching asteroid as seen from the camera on the ISS. The asteroid was rushing toward the lens, then the angle changed and the picture quickly rotated, showing a large fiery glow shooting through the atmosphere.

A moment later, a small plume of dark dirt spread out over the snow of the impact area, much farther west than anticipated. A billowing gray cloud suddenly erupted from the surface and the president turned to look at Grant, who was bringing out his phone. "What just happened?"

Grant covered the phone with his hand. "I'm trying to find out. Let's go to the situation room."

***

ISS:

Rhonda floated in numb silence with Vincent, John, Stacy, and Camilla looking over her shoulder. She was staring at the small eruption of gray ash, now spreading east across the snow-covered central plains of the United States. "John? You'd better call mission control and tell them we would like to get out of here in the emergency escape capsule real soon."

When John floated away, Rhonda turned back to her fellow astronauts and saw the fear in their eyes. "I'm sure the government has plans for this type of situation."

Camilla was still clutching her medallion and kissed it. "I just want to get back to my husband and children, before it is too late."

***

WASHINGTON D.C. THE WHITE HOUSE SITUATION ROOM:

President Brill sat down in the center chair at the oval table beside Patricia Winston, the Vice President, studying the six people taking their seats, then he looked over at one of his advisors. "Richard? Why don't you start by telling me what just happened?"

Richard Styles, a geophysicist, stood for a better view of the president. "Yes, Sir. The asteroid was more dense than anticipated and lost little of its mass as it passed through the atmosphere. Unfortunately, our computer model didn't account for that variable. It hit the Yellowstone caldera, which is a fifty-mile diameter pocket of molten rock just below the surface, and the impact caused a small eruption. For the moment we're lucky, Mister President. In case you didn't know, it could have been a super volcanic eruption."

"How long will it continue?"

"It's impossible to say, Sir. It could stop and nothing more happens, or it could keep erupting for a long time. Worst-case scenario? It's a prelude to the big one."

Brill looked along the table to his environmental advisor, Walter Moore. "Walt? Didn't something similar happen back in the fifteen hundreds?"

"Yes, Sir. A volcano in Iceland erupted with enormous force, and the ash blocked the sunlight in the northern hemisphere for a year and a half, killing most of the vegetation. Millions of people and most of the animals died from the famine and diseases it created. Fortunately, it only affected the northern hemisphere, but we may not be so lucky."

"Why is that?"

"If we have a super eruption, the poisonous gasses will contaminate the water, and fine dust particles will block the sunlight. The food chain will dissolve, causing mass starvation and disease. Anyone still alive will be fighting over anything left until the last person, animal, and insect dies."

Styles remained quiet while listening to the voice coming from his earbud, then raised his hand to get the President's attention. "Sir, I just received word from the USGS station in Yellowstone National Park. The impact forced the magma in the Yellowstone caldera to compress the magma deeper in the planet, which is causing seismic events along the Pacific Rim. Mister President, if these smaller volcanoes become active at the same time, it will affect the entire planet, just like a super eruption."

Grant touched the President's forearm. "We are much better prepared for something like this than they were in the fifteen hundreds. We should be okay."

Brill wasn't sure and turned back to Styles. "Is he correct?"

"No, Sir. Right now, the volcanoes along the Pacific Rim are still dormant, but that may not last. I believe the only way to stop them from erupting is to relieve the pressure."

The president's jaw dropped open for an instant. "You're kidding? How do you intend to do something that insane?"

"Not me, Mister President. I'm hoping a retired volcanologist I know can figure it out. His name is Marcus Hunter."

"When we're done here, do whatever it takes to get him in on this."

Environmental advisor Moore raised his hand to get the President's attention. "Sir, I think we should activate the WALNUT scenario. We already know we won't get them all, especially in the middle of winter. It's time they get moving, Sir."

Brill indicated to proceed with the plan, then looked over at Francis Wong, who was in charge of the Department of Energy. "How long will we be able to keep the power on?"

"That depends on how many eruptions occur and how soon, but I believe we will be okay for a while. Right now, the ash spreading east of Yellowstone is in a narrow band, which will block sunlight for solar energy along its path, but mechanically generated energy will continue until all the air filters are clogged. How far north or south the ash spreads will depend on the weather."

"What about west of the park?"

"Everything west of Yellowstone should be safe for several days, but again, it depends on the weather and how long it takes for the ash to circulate around the planet."

Brill thought about it for a moment, then looked at Styles. "Worst-case scenario?"

"The Yellowstone super volcano erupts and we all die. Even if we get lucky and it doesn't erupt, if more volcanoes become active, things will get bad. The nuclear reactors will work for a while, but they will have to be shut off before they overheat and melt down. We'll have from four days to a week, Sir, before everything on the surface of the Northern hemisphere goes dark."

Brill glanced up at the monitor showing the ash stream from the park, then over at Moore. "How long before the ash reaches us here at the White House?"

Moore studied his notes for a moment, then looked over at the President. "Depending on the jet stream, sometime tonight, Sir. That's my best estimate."

Grant stood up and looked down at the president. "Sir? I suggest we move you to Camp David."

Brill looked across at Admiral Turner. "I don't want people to think I'm a coward. Do you believe he's right?"

"Yes, Sir. That's the best place for you and your family. We'll handle everything out here for you, Mister President."

Brill looked over at the Vice President. "You're the best person to handle the people in the underground shelter, Pat. I'm sure we'll make it through this."

"I hope you're right, Sir, because it sounds like things are going to get real bad, and Fort Collins isn't that far from Yellowstone. Sir, you know how much I hate going underground."

"It's south of the eruption, so you should be okay."

"It's a military complex. Can't you send a general to be in charge?"

"No, Pat, the citizens must trust us, and knowing you're at the facility will add confidence their government can handle the situation."

When he saw Patricia was going to argue, Brill turned to his geophysics advisor. "Mister Styles, get Mister Hunter to Camp David as soon as possible and he can explain his plan. Is there anything else?"

Grant saw Styles was about to raise his hand and interrupted. "I'm sure you have a lot of questions the President can't answer. Contact the people who *can* answer them, and let us know what you find out."

When President Brill noticed everyone seemed to agree, he stood, as did all those in the room. "Good luck to all of you."

Brill headed for the exit, with Patricia and Grant right behind him. They continued along the hallway, then entered his office, where he indicated for them to sit down, but the VP remained standing. He closed the door before sitting on the edge of his desk. "Both of you should get to your families immediately before people panic and you can't make it. I'll set up the press conference."

Patricia folded her arms across her chest and stared at the President of the United States. "I don't want to go underground."

Brill knew how stubborn the forty-seven-year-old could be, and figured her feistiness was because of her small stature, but he had picked her as his running mate because she had nearly eight hundred thousand followers on social media, which he had needed to win the election. "I'm sorry, Pat, but that's where I need you right now."

Patricia gave Brill a nod of understanding before getting up and heading out the door, then he looked at Grant. "What about you, Mark?"

"I don't have any immediate family, and since my job takes up all my time, I don't have a girlfriend. I'll stay here with you and make the arrangements for the press conference."

"Thanks."

When Grant left the room, Brill moved around his desk and opened a cabinet door. He grabbed a decanter of blended whiskey, then poured a small amount into a glass and sat down behind his desk. He took a small sip, then pressed a contact on his telephone console. "Hi, Darling. You and the kids pack some clothes. We'll be leaving right away."

***

Styles was in the back seat of his government limo, leaving the White House as he called his personal secretary. "William, find out where Marcus Hunter lives and send a team to retrieve him. I want him at Camp David within five hours, is that clear? Good. Call me when you find him."

Styles opened a cabinet door and grabbed a small glass, then retrieved a bottle of brandy and poured two shots before replacing it. He grabbed the glass and leaned back in the seat, then took a large sip before looking out the window at the snow covering the ground and greenery. "I think we're screwed."

Chapter 3

HOSPITAL IN SPRINGFIELD, MISSOURI:

Jackson Atwater, a forty-three-year-old medical doctor specializing in hand and foot surgery, was coming out of the waiting area when a man wearing a suit and tie suddenly stood from a chair and stared at his approach. As the man reached into his coat pocket, Jackson stopped in front of him. "Can I help you?"

The man showed his United States Marshal Service badge and identification card. "Hello, Mister Atwater. I'm Ramon Choy, and I couldn't reach you on the phone. I came here to inform you the word of the day is Walnut."

Jackson indicated he understood and grabbed his coat off the rack, then led Ramon from the room and stopped at the receptionist. "I'll be gone for a few days."

Before she could ask questions, he and Ramon hurried out the front door. While Ramon climbed into a black sedan and drove away, Jackson climbed into his SUV and headed out of the parking lot.

***

CENTRAL HIGH SCHOOL:

Fifteen minutes later, Jackson stopped in front of the entrance and climbed out, then hurried up the steps and entered the building. He stopped at the security checkpoint and explained he had a family emergency and needed to get his daughter and son. He showed his ID to the guard, who checked the computer information for verification, then he was allowed through. He hurried along the corridors, checking room numbers until he found the first door, then knocked and entered.

Sixteen-year-old Nancy Atwater heard a knock on the door and turned to see her father enter the room. The teacher stopped speaking to see who it was as all the other students stared at him. She recognized the look in his eyes and immediately stood and grabbed her backpack, then hurried over to join him in the doorway. When she turned and looked at her friends, tears blurred her vision, so she spun around and left the room.

Jackson closed the door and grabbed his little girl's hand as they headed along the corridor to his son's classroom. He opened the door and entered, then looked around until he saw his eighteen-year-old son, Clark, who was staring at him. He gave Clark a slight nod, waiting while the young man got up and grabbed his backpack before hurrying to join him.

Once Clark was out of the room, Jackson saw the teacher's puzzled expression, but he closed the door and put his arm around his boy's shoulder as they headed for the exit. "Time to go."

Clark nearly stopped walking. "What about my car?"

Jackson knew his boy had worked hard to buy his older model Corvette. "I'm sorry, but it won't help us now."

When they strolled outside, Jackson led them to the SUV, where all three climbed in. After they left the school grounds, he got onto the highway to their home. He noticed the reflection in the rearview mirror of his son staring out the side window, then he looked over at Nancy. "We'll be okay."

She turned to look at her father. "I know, but what about mom?"

"She's on the secret Mars colony mission and there's no way for us to contact her. We stick to the plan."

Clark stared out the window as they drove past homes displaying holiday decorations. "I can't believe this is really happening."

"We knew there may come a time when I would be needed by the government. Just remember, we are under orders to tell no one about our final destination."

Jackson drove as if on autopilot, wondering what the emergency might be, knowing it must be very important. They never knew when a major event would happen and continued their lives without worrying about it. His biggest regret was not having his ex-wife and mother of his children with them on Earth.

Ten minutes later, Jackson stopped in the garage of their home and everyone climbed out. They entered the house and Jackson headed for his bedroom, while his kids headed to their own rooms to pack clothes and basic hygiene supplies. They took their backpacks into the garage and put everything into the back of the SUV, then added camping equipment. Once the pre-packed supplies were loaded, they went into the house for one last look around.

Nancy studied the family pictures on the walls. "We're never coming back, are we?"

Jackson put his hand on her shoulder. "I'm afraid not. Our lives are going to change in ways we can't even imagine."

The kids headed to the car while Jackson checked the lock on the front door and set the alarm system, then hurried into the garage. Since Clark was already behind the steering wheel, he got into the passenger seat beside him and they backed out of the garage. As Clark drove away, Jackson stared at the large door dropping into place, then at the decorations on the front lawn, knowing he would probably never see this home again.

Nancy had climbed into the back seat and scooted into the middle so she could see them in the rear-view mirror. "I'm already missing my friends."

Clark looked at her reflection. "Don't worry. Everyone likes you and you'll make new friends wherever we end up living." He glanced over at his dad. "Do you know what's going on?"

"All I know is there is going to be a worldwide catastrophe, and they need my help. My instructions are to get us to a massive underground complex set up for this type of situation. We'll take my plane and fly to Fort Collins, Colorado, where the government will take us the rest of the way to the underground facility just southwest of there."

When Jackson turned on the radio, everyone's attention was drawn to the announcer explaining what happened with the asteroid hitting Yellowstone. The announcer stated that even though there was no super eruption, if multiple smaller volcanoes erupt, it will affect most life in the northern hemisphere.

Jackson glanced over at Clark. "That answers our question. Let's hope we make it to Fort Collins before things get too bad."

***

COUNTY AIRPORT:

Jackson waited while Clark stopped the SUV outside the FAA office, then he got out and closed the door. He would file a flight plan while his kids loaded their gear into the plane, then he would join them when he was done. He watched his children drive away toward the planes tied down on the tarmac before entering the building.

He heard the phone ringing while the woman in charge was already talking to someone on another line, so he waited. The view out the window showed people standing around several planes, all being readied for flight by a few of the local people.

Jean ended the call and ignored the ringing. "Hey, Jackson. I didn't expect to see you here today."

"Hi, Jean. Sounds like a busy day."

"Sure is. What can I do for you?"

"I need to file a flight plan to Fort Collins, Colorado."

"Sure thing, but watch out. Headquarters issued a warning about the ash from the eruption, and they're shutting down the airports in the central eastern half of the country."

"I appreciate it."

She indicated the ringing phone. "You'd better get going while you can, because I have a feeling they'll be shutting us down before too much longer."

"Thanks for the heads up."

Jackson filed the flight plan and left the building, then hurried along the tarmac in front of the hangars, where a few people inside were getting their planes ready to leave. As he passed the last structure, he saw his SUV parked next to his twin engine Cessna and joined his kids.

Cark put his hand on the door handle of the SUV. "I'll park behind the hangars and be right back."

Nancy was waiting at the bottom of the stairs up into the aircraft and got up as her father stopped. "A man came by looking for a ride and I said no. I didn't want to go into details in case he tells someone else, so he went into one of the hangars to look for a ride. Here comes Clark. I'll start the preflight check."

"Great. I'm glad you got your pilot's license and I don't have to do all the flying."

"Are you kidding? You love to fly as much as I do."

When Nancy climbed the stairs into the plane, Jackson watched Clark jogging across the tarmac. When he stopped in front of him, he was amazed his son was not out of breath. "Let's get out of here."

Jackson got in first and left Clark to close the hatch as he went up the aisle and climbed into the copilot's seat. When Clark got into the seat behind him, Jackson looked over at his daughter, who was flipping switches.

Nancy started the first engine, studying the gauges as she set the speed to idle. The second engine started, and the readouts showed both engines were purring.

She slid the headset on and moved the microphone in front of her mouth, then spoke to the air traffic controller. She released the brakes and increased the throttles, then followed the instructions and steered onto the familiar taxi way. When she reached the end of the first runway, she stopped to look around for any other aircraft, then set the throttles to full and released the brakes.

Everyone was pushed back into their seats as the propellers grabbed the air and the plane gained speed along the runway. When the airspeed reached eighty knots, Nancy eased back on the yoke, forcing the plane into the air. She banked the aircraft to the left as the plane continued gaining altitude, spiraling up above the airport.

When she leveled off at ten thousand feet, they saw the billowing cloud of ash from Yellowstone rising forty thousand feet into the atmosphere. The gray column blocked some of the sky, with a dark tail flowing east over the northern great plains of the central United States.

***

WESTERN KANSAS:

Hundreds of private and commercial aircraft were headed south, and the control towers were being overwhelmed. Commercial airliners searching for places to land and refuel took priority, leaving the private pilots to follow standard operating procedures on their own, but it was not working as planned. Faster planes were flying over or under the slower aircraft, all perpendicular to the Jackson's flight path west.

Nancy had an idea. "I'll drop us down to three thousand feet and we can avoid all this traffic. Check for anyone flying below us."

Jackson stared out the side window while Clark moved to the back of the aircraft and strained to see below, informing Nancy they did not see anything, then the plane quickly descended below the rest of the airplanes. Clark saw another craft an instant before one of its landing wheels clipped the tail rudder of their plane and veered away.

Nancy strained to control a frozen left-hand turn, searching for a wide enough space in the forest below for a crash landing. The propellers ripped branches from trees as the plane flipped sideways, cartwheeling through the forest.

***

When Clark opened his eyes and saw an exit sign, he realized he was lying on the floor in the tail of the aircraft. He tried to push himself up, but intense pain erupted in his left shoulder as the dislocation popped back into place. The last thing he remembered was watching the propellers chopping off the treetops before one wing snagged a trunk, causing the plane to cartwheel through the forest until breaking in half.

He checked his wristwatch and saw it was nearly 1:00 PM. As his thoughts cleared, he realized he had been unconscious for half an hour. He grabbed the hand bar near the rear exit hatch with his right hand to pull himself off the floor, then cradled his left arm while staring out through the ragged edges of the aluminum fuselage, just forward of the wing mounts.

When he stepped outside into a trench in the dirt where the cockpit should be, he saw it lying among the tree trunks fifty feet away. "No!" he yelled as he hurried across to find his family.

***

Jackson reached up to his forehead, feeling a knot and liquid on his fingers. He looked over at his daughter with her chin resting on her chest, but when he tried to get up, was held in place by his restraint. He jabbed the release button and turned in his seat, then reached over to check her neck for a pulse. He sighed with relief when he found it, then placed a hand on her shoulder. "Nancy? Can you hear me, sweetheart?"

Nancy raised her head to look over at her father. "I'm okay, but your head is bleeding."

He smiled. "Yeah, but we're alive."

She released her harness and turned in her chair to face him for an instant before noticing the rest of the plane was missing. "Shit! Where's Clark?"

Jackson leaned back as Nancy shoved him out of the way and ran out of the plane. He smiled when he saw Clark headed in their direction, but as he stood up, felt lightheaded and clung to the back of his seat for balance. Once it passed, he stepped out to join his children, giving Clark a hug. "I'm glad you're alive, Son. What happened to your arm?"

"A separated shoulder, but it's back in place now. When I saw the plane was ripped apart, I thought both of you were dead."

Jackson looked around the area. "We're still alive, but all our gear must be somewhere along our route."

Clark indicated the back half of the plane. "The forward cargo compartment was ripped opened, but the one in the rear section is still intact."

"What do we have back there?"

"Mostly our packaged goods for the trip."

Nancy stared across at the rear half of the plane. "At least we're alive."

Jackson noticed the glistening on the leaves of the trees. "We're lucky this area is still wet from a recent snowstorm and nothing caught fire. Nancy and I will go get our gear while you stay here and guard our supplies."

"That's going to be difficult without my gun. It's in my backpack."

"That's okay. I keep a thirty-eight caliber pistol in a small compartment in the cockpit. I'll be right back."

Nancy found a piece of window curtain and ripped it to size, then wrapped it around Clark's left forearm and shoulder as a sling. "My gun is in my pack, too. How long have you been awake?"

"Just now, but we've all been unconscious for half an hour."

When Jackson returned, Clark reached out and accepted the gun. "You might need it while you're searching."

Jackson put his boot up on a log and raised his pant leg to expose the small gun in a holster around his ankle. "I've got it covered."

Nancy looked over at Clark. "We shouldn't be gone too long."

Jackson slid his pistol from his ankle holster and put it into his front pocket. "Let's go."

Clark felt the light weight of the pistol in his hand. It was advertised as an air weight, at about two ounces, and he slid it into the crux of his sling. He returned to the fuselage, then sat in a broken chair to watch his family head back through the broken branches.

When they moved out of sight, he listened to the sound of them stepping on branches as they headed back along the trail of broken tree limbs. The sound faded to nothing, until a few minutes later, when he heard a distinct sound coming from a different direction. He reached into his sling to place his hand on the gun, then a large horse with an elderly woman on its back snorted as it stepped into the new small clearing.

The woman stayed on the horse and guided it to the stranger. "I'm surprised to see someone alive. I'm Barbara Sterling, and this is my land."

"I'm Clark Atwater. Sorry to trespass, but we didn't have a choice."

"We?"

"Yeah, my father and sister are searching for our gear."

Barbara studied the fuselage, then looked over at the cockpit for a moment before turning to Clark. "You're lucky. Did you break your arm?"

"No, just separated my shoulder."

When the woman got off the horse and turned to face him, he saw her holster and revolver. When she moved to one of the undamaged chairs and sat down across from him, he slid his hand out of his sling onto the armrest.

Barbara was relieved when the boy placed his hand out in the open. "Where are you coming from?"

"Springfield, Missouri. We were headed toward Fort Collins when another plane clipped our tail rudder and we lost control."

"I'm surprised to hear that happened. There usually isn't much air traffic over this area."

"The sky got crowded when everyone decided to head south because of the eruption."

Clark heard a breaking tree branch just as Barbara stood, then he saw Jackson and Nancy approaching with the backpacks. When he saw Barbara's hand moving toward her pistol, he got up and stood in her way. "Don't worry. That's my dad and sister."

Jackson stopped in front of the stranger and set Clark's backpack on the ground, then slid his pack from his shoulders. "Hello. That's a nice-looking horse."

"Thanks. I'm Barbara and that's Sam. I understand you're headed to Fort Collins?"

"That's right. I'm Jackson Atwater, and this is my daughter, Nancy. You already know Clark. We could use some help with directions."

Barbara studied the supplies, camp gear, and backpacks, then turned to Jackson. "It's about a hundred and twenty miles as the crow flies, but you won't get there from here. Is this everything?"

"Everything worth salvaging."

"Okay. I'll take you to a road and you can get your bearings."

"Great."

"Find a sack or something to put your stuff in, and I'll sling it over Sam's saddle."

While Nancy and Clark searched for bags, Jackson smiled at Barbara. "We really appreciate it."

"I don't suppose you'll get the wreckage off my land."

"I can't make any promises, but I'll try to get someone in Fort Collins to help you."

"Fair enough. I appreciate your honesty. You should know the ash is spreading further south now. A lot of folks are heading away from it, so there are no vehicles left in the valley."

"Then I guess we're walking."

Chapter 4

ISS:

Inside the station, no one wanted to work. They just stared out the windows at the narrow band of gray ash and brown dust moving east across the north central United States, and the spears of lightning created by static electricity visible in the haze.

John floated into the room and grabbed a handle on the wall to stop. "Mission control agreed to let us return to Earth, but on such short notice, they may not reach us right away. Let's grab our belongings and get out of here."

Everyone floated toward the living section of the station to grab their personal belongings. Mostly they were pictures of family and friends, but some of them stopped to grab their research materials, blocking the way of the others wanting to get to the escape capsule.

Rhonda forced her way past Camilla, Stacy, and John, and was first to arrive at the small room where they stored the spacesuits. Since it was near the airlock into the escape capsule, she set her small backpack aside to put on her suit, then looked over as Vincent entered with his little suitcase. "I take it you don't have much to take home, either."

Vincent patted the four inch by six inch bulge in his shirt pocket, and the object on a short chain around his neck. "My bible and cross are the only things I will need." He set his pack down while he put on his suit. "God almighty will protect and guide me through the trying times ahead of us."

It suddenly sounded like bullets were hitting the station as alarms blared. Rhonda and Vincent quickly put on their helmets and air packs, then entered the escape capsule. Rhonda remained near the open hatch into the station, while frantically waving for her floating companions to hurry, but it was too late. They stopped moving, with their last breaths frozen into frost on their lips, noses, and eyelashes.

Rhonda turned around and looked into the escape capsule, where Vincent was strapping himself into one of the chairs. She tossed a portable radio inside and closed the hatch, then turned on the power and set the environmental controls. Once she entered a command into the system, a computer generated voice told them to stand by for separation, counting down from three.

When the voice said zero, Rhonda looked out through the small window and saw they were drifting away from the station. As they headed toward the atmosphere, the view showed ragged sheets of punctured metal and smashed solar panels around the ISS. "It must have been hit by micro asteroids left over from the explosion."

Her heart broke when she saw the bodies of their companions floating among the debris. "Come over here to look at this."

Vincent remained in his chair. "Why? We know they are dead. It was God who saved me, so it must be for a divine purpose. Perhaps they are dead because they did not believe in his almighty power, and the only reason you are still alive is because he wants me to save your soul."

Rhonda decided not to indulge or argue with him and continued looking out the window. When he had interacted with the crew, she had seen no signs of him being overly religious, but now his tone of voice was verging on fanatical.

When the computer voice told them to prepare for reentry, Rhonda sat down and strapped into her harness. A few seconds later, the capsule began shaking as they entered the atmosphere, while yellow flames blocked the view outside the window. After a few tense moments, the shaking stopped, and the flames vanished, but they still felt nearly weightless as the capsule continued plummeting back to Earth.

They were suddenly pushed down into their seats as the orange and white striped parachutes filled with air. A few moments later, the capsule shuddered as it hit the water.

***

PACIFIC OCEAN. *WINDANCER***:**

Rickie stepped out from below onto the main deck to enjoy the aroma of the ocean and the wind in her hair. When she noticed Geneva lying on a recliner in the sun, she strolled over to join her. "You haven't said much since we left San Diego, and eating alone in your cabin isn't helping you get to know us. You must be enjoying some part of this trip."

Geneva remained prone while looking up through her sunglasses at her cousin, then tossed her cigarette butt over the railing. "First, Marcus drags me away from my friends, then wants me to quit smoking. Now I'm trapped on this boat with people I hardly know, and I can't get any bars on my phone. How am I supposed to survive without any bars?"

Rickie smirked at her. "Why are you worried about bars? You're too young to drink."

Geneva lifted her sunglasses to look into her cousin's eyes. "You think that's funny? I managed to buy wine in Reno with a fake ID."

"Good for you. How did you like our stop in Acapulco yesterday? Did you have a margarita?"

"I don't know what that is. They didn't have my brand of cigarettes, and said I couldn't get them until we get to Lima, Peru. And I'm not enjoying being stuck out here on the ocean with nothing to do." She lowered the sunglasses and closed her eyes.

Rickie slid a deck chair into the shade of the sail and sat down. She was staring at the western horizon when three orange and white parachutes suddenly appeared and dropped toward the ocean a few miles away. She got up and hurried up the steps into the pilothouse to join Marcus. "Did you see the parachutes?"

"No. Which direction?"

"A few miles due west. I think it was a spacecraft returning from orbit."

Marcus grabbed the binoculars and scanned the western waters. "I don't see any support ships or helicopters."

"There were three chutes attached to one object, so I can't imagine what else it could be. If there are astronauts on board, they won't last long and we should go check it out."

Marcus entered the coordinates into the navigation computer, then the ship began to turn. The sails became limp as they lost the wind, then the booms swung across the deck and the sails snapped taught as they headed west.

Rickie grabbed the binoculars and searched for the spacecraft. Olivia joined them while they studied the horizon, and even Geneva was standing and looking for the parachutes. When they reached the approximate area where she saw them hit the water, there was no floating spacecraft, so Rickie lowered her binoculars.

Geneva looked up into the window of the pilothouse. "Whatever it was, maybe it sank."

***

ISS ESCAPE CAPSULE:

Rhonda released her harness and tried to stand up, but after five months in zero gravity, her legs didn't want to support her weight right away, and she collapsed onto the floor. She looked up at Vincent, who was still in his seat. When he didn't offer to help her get up, she crawled to the control console and straightened up onto her knees to grab the microphone. "Mission control, this is ISS escape capsule. Come in, please. Mission control, this is the ISS escape capsule. Can anyone hear me?"

When no one replied, she crawled over to the escape hatch and grabbed the handle. She struggled with the lever, but could not get it open.

Vincent knew if they opened the hatch before help arrived, water could enter, and they could sink. "What are you doing?"

"We need to get the hatch open and find out where we are."

"Will the support team not pull the capsule onto a ship?"

"We're on our own now, so get up and help me open the hatch."

"Then what do we do?"

"There should be a life raft in here someplace. We find it and get outside where we can try to figure out where we landed. The GPS shows we're off the coast of Peru. Maybe it's within rowing distance."

"What is the point? I cannot walk any better than you can. If God decided this is our time to join him, why fight it?"

"If we don't start adapting to gravity, we'll die in this can, with or without divine intervention, so get your ass up and start using your muscles."

Vincent watched Rhonda slide across the floor to the cabinets. As she began opening doors, he released his harness and used his arms to push his body up out of the chair to stand up. He held on as his legs wobbled, but since he had only been weightless for fifteen days, he managed to keep them straight to support his weight.

Rhonda grabbed the cabinet handle and pulled her body up until she was standing, then cautiously took a step along the wall. When she opened the cabinet door next to the hatch, she saw an orange life raft strapped inside. She released the clip, and it fell free, but when she grabbed it with one hand, she didn't have the strength to hang on and it hit the floor.

Vincent held onto the wall for balance as he moved around the room to join Rhonda at the hatch, then together they managed to get it open. They tossed the raft out through the opening, then Rhonda pulled the cord to inflate it. The hissing of escaping compressed gas drowned out any other sounds until the raft reached its full size, then everything seemed deathly quiet.

Rhonda tumbled out from the capsule into the raft, then moved to one side as she looked around the vast expanse of open water. There was no land in view from her side of the capsule, and a stiff breeze was pushing them west into the vast Pacific Ocean.

Vincent remained inside the capsule, looking out at the horizon. "Since we seem to be floating okay, I think we should stay in here until our muscles get used to operating in this environment. At least we will have a solid surface."

Rhonda crawled back into the capsule and carefully stood up while hanging onto the wall for support. "Good idea. Let's check to see what we have for survival."

***

WINDANCER:

Everyone but Marcus was out on the open deck, searching for the parachutes, when Geneva suddenly shaded her eyes with both hands. "We're looking for something orange, right?"

Rickie swung the binoculars toward Geneva's gaze. "I see it, too." She looked up at Marcus through the open window as she pointed southwest. "Over there, Grandpa."

Marcus looked in the direction Rickie was pointing and saw the orange object, but when they headed that way, the sails lost the wind. He pressed the button to bring them down, and they were automatically rolled into the booms, then he started the engines and headed for the orange dot.

When his ship was within two hundred feet of the orange raft, he saw the open hatch of the capsule and put the propellers in neutral to let the momentum silently drive it closer. When the *Windancer* was alongside, he put the propellers into reverse for a moment to stop.

Rickie was near the bow as the ship stopped alongside the raft. "Ahoy. Is anyone alive?"

Vincent heard a strange voice and carefully turned around, then smiled at the young lady on the deck of a ship. "Yes! By the grace of God almighty, we are here. Can you help us?"

While Olivia moved up beside her, Rickie shaded her eyes and stared into the opening of the capsule. "Yes, but I can't see you. Move closer to the door."

Vincent moved to the opening. "You do not know how glad I am to see you."

Rhonda moved up beside Vincent and waved at the woman and young lady staring at her. "He means *we* are both glad to see you. We just escaped from the International Space Station before it was destroyed."

Olivia gave them a quizzical stare. "What do you mean?"

Vincent was eager to get out. "We will explain what happened, but first, let us onto your ship before this escape capsule sinks."

"Of course. Get into your raft and row over while I lower the ladder."

Rhonda grinned up at Olivia. "That might be a problem. We've been weightless for a while and our legs and arms are not working as good as they should."

"Right. If you can crawl into your raft, we'll toss you a line and pull you over, then help you on board."

While Vincent moved through the opening into the raft, Rhonda grabbed the portable custom radio she had saved from the station. She handed it to Vincent, then stepped through the opening and collapsed onto the floor of the raft. When she realized Vincent was not going to help, she got onto her knees and held her arms out, then caught the rope tossed by the girl and wrapped it around the rubber cleat.

Rickie hauled on the line until the raft was even with the short rope ladder. She used a boat hook to hold it in place, while Olivia knelt on the deck and reached down to take Rhonda's hand to help her stand up. Geneva knelt beside Olivia, reaching down to take Rhonda's other hand as they hauled her onto the deck.

Marcus was standing outside the pilothouse, watching the progress of the rescue. When he saw the ladies struggling to haul the woman out of the raft, he hurried down the stairs just as she got onboard. He wrapped his arm around Rhonda's waist while draping her arm over his shoulder to help her walk, then led her away from the girls to one of the deck chairs and lowered her onto the seat. "Are you okay?"

"Yes, I just don't have my land legs yet. Or should I say, sea legs."

He smiled. "I'm Marcus Hunter, and this is my ship."

"I'm Rhonda Pryor. Thanks for coming to our rescue."

"If you hadn't inflated your raft, we would have missed you and continued on."

Vincent looked up at the deck and saw a pretty young girl with a tattooed arm, then he smiled as he held the radio out to her. "Would you mind taking this for me?"

Geneva felt a chill run up her spine as she recognized the leering look in the stranger's eyes. She had been fighting off men like him since she was twelve, and they had not gotten her yet. She cautiously moved forward and held out her hand.

When the girl reached out and grabbed the radio, Vincent studied her tattoo before letting go. "I like your art."

She took the radio and stepped back. "Whatever."

Vincent looked up at the other two women as they grabbed his hands. He clumsily climbed the rungs onto the deck, then the older woman helped him hobble over to a chair and he sat down. "May God bless you for saving me."

Marcus moved back to the railing and noticed Geneva holding a large portable radio he didn't recognize. He grabbed the line on the small orange raft and walked it to the stern to tie it off. When he returned to the main deck, he saw Rickie handing out bottles of water to their new guests. "Let's get back to the part about you escaping from the ISS."

Rhonda took a few swallows of water before speaking. "After we watched the eruption, we were getting ready to go back to Earth when we were hit by a micro asteroid shower. I figured they were left over from the missile explosion of the asteroid. We were close to the escape capsule and barely managed to get inside before the air and heat escaped from the station. The others weren't so lucky."

Marcus wasn't sure he had heard correctly. "Hold on a second. What eruption?"

Rhonda told them about the impact in Yellowstone. "Right after that, we were hit by the micro asteroids."

Marcus slumped onto one of the chairs. "I wrote a research paper on the aftereffects of a Yellowstone super eruption, and the outcome is bad. It will kill all life on the planet."

"Right now, it is only a minor eruption in Yellowstone and maybe it will stop, but we don't know if any more have erupted around the world."

Olivia wrapped her arm around Rickie's waist and held her close. "Dad, we should head back to California."

"No, our best chance for survival is in the southern hemisphere. That's why I have a boat."

When Marcus got up and climbed the steps to the pilothouse, Vincent noticed the tattooed girl still holding the radio. "What's your name?"

"Geneva Hunter. Marcus is my grandfather."

Olivia was listening. "I'm Doctor Olivia Hunter, and Marcus is my father. This is my niece, and that's my daughter, Rickie."

"I am Vincent Cristallis. I am really glad God put me on this path to meet all of you."

Rhonda grabbed the railing and stood to get used to the gravity. "Thanks for saving our lives."

"We were lucky my daughter was looking in the right direction to see your parachutes, or we would never have known you were here."

Vincent held his gaze on Geneva before looking at Olivia. "It is God's will that you found us. Let us pray together for his almighty power?"

Vincent reached out to Rickie with one hand, but she didn't accept and took a step away from him. When Olivia folded her arms over her chest, he reached out to Geneva.

Geneva stepped back from Vincent's hand and glared at him. "That's your thing, not mine. Just leave me alone."

Through the open side window in the pilothouse, Marcus heard Vincent's request and Geneva's reaction. He grabbed the microphone for the public address system and pressed the button on the side. "Stand by to come about and raise the sails."

Vincent looked around. "What does he mean, come about?"

Rhonda sat down. "It means don't stand up."

While the ship turned southeast, Vincent watched in amazement as the sails were automatically raised. The ship continued to turn and the three ladies instinctively ducked as the mainsail boom swung across the deck, missing the top of Vincent's head by two feet before billowing with air. He felt the increase in speed, then the low rumble from the exhaust roiling out of the water at the stern was suddenly gone, leaving only the whisper of the wind in the rigging. He grabbed the railing and pulled himself out of the chair to stand up. "I have never done this before, and it is amazing."

Marcus stepped out of the pilothouse and looked out at his family helping the astronauts down into the ship. "Welcome aboard the *Windancer*."

When they disappeared below, Marcus strolled back into the pilothouse and checked the computer monitor to make sure they were headed for Lima, Peru. He checked the radar for any vessels in the area, but there were none within range. He reached down into a small refrigerator and grabbed a beer, then thought about the future, frowning as he opened the cap and took a sip.

Chapter 5

WINDANCER:

The sun was directly overhead as Olivia stepped into the pilothouse from the inside stairs, then sat in a captain's chair next to Marcus. A radio news broadcast was playing through the intercom speakers of the ship, and she continued to listen to a woman announcer in Hawaii. She was describing the Mauna Loa and Kilauea volcanoes spewing more magma than ever recorded, causing mass evacuations from the path of the lava and burning vegetation.

The announcer introduced a male journalist, who was taking over the broadcast from southeastern Idaho in the United States. He was talking about the Yellowstone eruption, which was creating earthquakes in the surrounding states. Most of them were in the 2.5 to 3.1 magnitude range, but early this morning, they were increasing from the 3.4 to 4.2 range. No one was certain if it meant Yellowstone is building up to a super eruption, or if the seismic events will continue to get worse. The band of ash has now spread to the eastern coast of North America, from Norfolk, Virginia to Baltimore, Maryland. It is heading out over the Atlantic Ocean, and expected to hit Europe in twelve hours.

Marcus took a sip of beer before looking over at his daughter. "I believe the quakes are relieving the pressure for now, but eventually, one side will win the battle, and I think both outcomes will be devastating."

"I hope the earthquakes win. At least the damage will be limited to the western side of North America and not the entire planet."

"I imagine people are already panicking. I know from experience, once the food begins to run out, people will kill to survive."

"What about all the dry goods we're carrying? They should last for a while."

Marcus grabbed the cargo manifest from a tray near the chart cabinet. "We have two hundred pounds of brown rice, three hundred and fifty pounds of white beans, and four hundred pounds of dehydrated potato flakes." He looked up and grinned at her. "And two pallets of dehydrated gourmet foods? I suppose you ordered those."

"I was impressed when I tried one last summer." She stopped when Geneva and Rickie ran into the pilothouse. "What's going on?"

Geneva put her hands on her hips as she glared at Marcus. "We heard the news, and this is just freaking great! Everyone is going to die and I'm stuck out here with people I hate instead of being with my friends."

When Geneva stomped out of the room and down the steps to the main deck, Olivia turned to Marcus. "I don't understand why she hates me."

"It's actually just me, so don't take it personally."

Rickie glanced out the window and down at Geneva, walking between the hatch covers, then headed for the inside stairs. "I'll go back down to the galley and clean up from lunch."

When Rickie headed down the stairs into the ship, Olivia looked out the front window and saw Geneva sitting on a hatch cover while smoking a cigarette. "Do you think she'll ever accept us as family?"

"We had a conversation last evening, and I think we're growing on her."

"Oh yeah? What did you talk about?"

"Thomas. She still hates him."

***

Down in the galley, Rickie noticed Rhonda and Vincent were still sitting at the table and began gathering the dirty dishes. "Don't worry about Geneva's little outburst. She'll be fine, but that means it's my turn to clean up."

Rhonda started to get out of her chair. "I'll give you a hand."

"No, sit back down. You'll get your chance once you know your way around a little better."

Vincent got up from the table, wearing jeans and a shirt on loan from Marcus, but they were too large, and he had to roll the cuffs up. "Thank you again for rescuing us."

Rhonda stared after Vincent until he disappeared from the room, then watched Rickie carry the plates to the sink and fill the dishwasher. "Thanks for letting me borrow some of your clothes."

"Sure. Some of my mom's stuff should work for you, too. Her cup size is only slightly larger than yours."

"That's one advantage to having small breasts. I can go braless most of the time." They exchanged grins. "Your grandfather has a nice boat, and it appears to be new."

"It was custom-built for him three years ago out of carbon fiber and aluminum, and everything in her is top of the line."

"He doesn't act like he's rich."

Rickie turned to look at Rhonda. "I know, and he doesn't realize he's good looking, either."

"What's the deal with Geneva?"

"My uncle Tom got her mom pregnant in their senior year of high school. The thing is, he didn't like her in that way, because she was a bit of a whore, but they were both drunk and shit happened. He married her right after they graduated, then he joined the Air Force to support them."

"He took responsibility? That's good. What happened?"

"From what I remember, Geneva really loved him, but when she was about seven, her mom, Aunt Helen, started drinking a lot. Tom wanted her to quit and I guess they were fighting whenever he was home, so he was asking to get deployed a lot more often. It turned out Helen was still a whore, and when he was gone, she was spending the nights at other men's houses. That's when Geneva started hating him for leaving all the time."

"Do they still talk?"

"Not anymore. Tom came back for a brief visit seven years ago, and Geneva blamed him for destroying her life. He went back overseas and was killed on a mission two weeks later, and a month after that, her mom was out drinking and killed herself in a car wreck. Geneva couldn't support herself and moved in with Aunt Helen's parents in Reno."

"That must have been tough on her."

"She tries to hide it by acting tough. We all went to the funeral, and at the reception, Geneva's grandparents got drunk. All of us thought it was because of their loss, but later, Grandpa learned they were heavy drinkers, and he found out Geneva was hanging out with the wrong type of friends all the time. After she got the tattoo, Grandpa was worried about how her life would end up, and filed for custody. He won, and she arrived in San Diego a couple of days ago. That's when my mom and I flew out to join them on this trip. We thought it might help her get used to grandpa."

"I take it that's not going well."

"I'm sure she'll change. I know what it was like at that age."

"Yeah, me, too. Do you mind if I ask how old you are?"

"Nope. Do you mind if I ask how old you are?"

Rhonda grinned. "I'm thirty."

"I'll be eighteen in three days. That's why I enjoy going on these trips with grandpa every summer. We always go someplace new to celebrate my birthday."

"Where's your father?"

"I have no idea. My mom is a medical doctor and didn't have time for a relationship, and used a donor from a sperm bank. We don't know who he is or was, but mom showed me his resume, and he had a lot of good features, including an IQ of one-sixty five."

"I guess you're very smart. Have you ever been curious about who he is?"

"Not seriously. Grandpa has been like a father to me, and that's all I need."

"How old is he?"

"Fifty-six, and my mom is forty-eight. How old is Vincent?"

"Fifty three, I think. It's hard to believe the space station is gone."

Rickie leaned back against the counter. "Everything is going to change now. I'm just glad to be out here on the ocean with my family and not in a crowded city. If there's no space program, what are you and Vincent going to do now?"

"I guess it depends on what happens next."

"It's the same with us."

When neither of them spoke for a few moments, Rickie turned on the dishwasher. "I'm going to find Geneva and make sure she's all right."

When Rickie left the galley, Rhonda listened to the quiet whirring of the dishwasher while thinking about her future. For the moment, she felt lucky to be on the *Windancer*, but also knew that could change as soon as they reached a port.

***

Vincent arrived at the top of the inside stairs into the pilothouse and saw Olivia was on watch. "I thought I would come up to see what goes on in here. This looks like the bridge of a regular ship."

"Pretty much, except this is a motorsailer, so we have two control systems. One for the propellers and one for the sails."

"Yes, that was amazing watching the sails open. I guess you do not need a big crew to haul them up."

"Or bring them down. Marcus makes most of his trips alone."

"Really? You and the girls are not part of the crew?"

"No, we go with him during the summer for the adventure."

"Is this his business?"

"It's just a hobby. He's a volcanologist, but one day he had this great idea for a new seismic sensor. He took on a partner, and together they built a startup business into a multi-million dollar company, then he sold his shares to enjoy life. He loves sailing and had this ship custom built."

"I am not trying to be nosey, but does he live on this boat full time?"

"Of course not. He could, but he has a house in the Smokey Mountains of North Carolina. I guess I should say he had a home there."

"I doubt I will ever return to my country. You said you are a doctor. What type?"

"I'm a medical doctor and have a general practice in Salem, Oregon."

"It looks like we might be stuck together for a while."

"Perhaps, but let me make this clear. I'm not interested."

"Okay, but I am not interested in you that way, either. I just thought I might be on this ship for a while and maybe I can help. I was thinking you should show me how all these controls work."

"Good. Let's start with the electronics."

***

Marcus was sitting in a reclining chair in the salon, thumbing through a magazine when Rickie walked in and sat across from him, so he looked over at her. "You look worried. What's going on?"

"I can't find Geneva. I've searched the entire ship and there is no sign of her. She was very upset when she heard the news earlier, and I'm worried she might have fallen overboard."

"I doubt it. Okay, I might know where she is."

"Tell me and I'll go get her."

"That's all right. We're still getting to know each other."

Marcus stood and set the magazine on the end table. "I'm glad you're keeping an eye on her for me."

Marcus left the salon and continued along the walkway through the center of the ship toward the stern, then past the four guest cabins to the door at the end and entered his bedroom. The room was illuminated by a window in the stern bulkhead, reflecting off the polished wood paneling. On one side of the large room, next to his desk, was a door to a bathroom, and on the other side was his bed and a closet.

He opened the closet door and saw his clothes shoved to one side of the pole. He reached in and pressed a tiny button hidden in the scrollwork of the wood trim. When the floor of the closet dropped down a few inches and slid to one side, he stepped in and went down the ladder.

When he reached the bottom, he stepped off onto the deck of a ten-foot square room below his bedroom. A three foot square door in the stern bulkhead was open, where Geneva was sitting on the ledge in front of it, staring out at the water behind the ship. "I see you found my secret room. What do you think?"

Geneva took a drag on a cigarette, then blew the smoke out through the opening. "I'm trying not to."

Marcus slowly moved closer to the doorway and stared out at the water. "In the old days, they called this a smuggler's hold. They used them for all kinds of reasons, but I had this one built as an escape in case I run into trouble I can't get out of by myself."

She threw the cigarette butt out through the opening. "Oh yeah? That isn't the only reason. I found your marijuana stash. It's not bad."

Marcus's jaw dropped open for a moment. "How in hell did you find this room in the first place? You can't see the door from the outside."

"From the size. I knew there was a space under your bedroom and there was no other way to get into it. I tried to find a way down in the bathroom, and when that didn't work, I tried the closet and was admiring the woodwork when I saw the button."

"What about my stash? There is no way you could have seen that hidden wall panel."

"You're right. I followed the smell coming from behind it. Are you going to lecture me about smoking it?"

"Of course not, but I have a piece of advice, and you can take it or leave it. The key is moderation. I only smoke it when I don't have anything dangerous to do later."

"But you drink a lot of beer while we're sailing. Isn't that the same thing?"

"I don't drink as much as you think, and it's not the same type of high. It's much less intense and doesn't hit all at once." He could tell she wasn't going to listen to him. "I wanted to let you know we're only five miles from shore, and you might get cell phone reception."

Marcus staggered back as Geneva rushed past him up the ladder. Once she was out of sight, he pressed one of the eight-inch-square wall panels and it opened. He studied the contents, then grinned when he realized she had not smoked it. He closed the panel and shut the small door out onto the stern, then headed up the ladder to his bedroom.

***

Rickie was below deck in the walkway when Geneva suddenly rushed past her and up the stairs onto the main deck. A moment later, Marcus strolled out of his cabin and stopped in front of her. "Where was she?"

"In my smugglers' hold."

"Oh, right. I forgot all about it. I'm surprised she found it."

"She's smarter than she appears."

He noticed the corner of the strange radio behind a stack of deck chair pillows and pointed it out to her. "Do you know what that does?"

Rickie grabbed the radio. "No. Let's go find out."

Chapter 6

CAMP DAVID:

President Brill was sitting at the head of a large round table, looking at his advisors, Mark Grant, Admiral James Turner, Walter Moore, and Francis Wong, then his gaze settled on geophysicist Richard Styles. "How is your plan to stop more eruptions coming along, Richard? From what I hear, nobody knows how to do it."

Styles looked up from his notepad. "It was just an idea, Sir. I didn't say I could do it. Only that I would try to find the only person who might know if it's possible."

"That would be your friend, Mister Hunter?"

"Yes, Sir. We haven't found him anywhere in the United States, but my people learned he runs cargo from San Diego to Peru, and they are searching the western coasts for his ship."

"Have any more volcanoes erupted?"

"Yes, Sir. Mauna Loa and Kilauea, in Hawaii. Fortunately, they are only expelling flowing magma, and it is not adding to the ash problem. Only toxic gasses in localized areas."

"That's good news. Will that relieve the pressure on the rest of them?"

"It's too soon to say, Sir."

Brill looked down the table at Wong. "What about power here in the US?"

"Ninety-seven percent of the power grid is still online, but the independent power stations in the path of the ash are shutting down because they're running out of clean air filters. Transportation is becoming a problem across the central plains states, because the truckers can't drive in the ash to deliver fuel."

"We knew it would happen. What about our underground facility in Fort Collins?"

"The military is dealing with unwanted civilians trying to get in, but so far it's still secure."

The emergency line rang, so Grant put the caller on speaker. "Go ahead."

"Mister President, you have a call from the Mars Colony. They're patching it through to your phone. Go ahead, Sir."

Brill leaned in toward the microphone. "This is the President speaking. Who am I talking to?"

"Marshal Barkley, Sir, the colony leader. We were wondering how things are going on Earth?"

"Not good, Mister Barkley. There are smaller disturbances in volcanoes happening all over the northern hemisphere, and if they go, things are going to become much worse than predicted."

"I'm sorry to hear that, Sir."

"My people say if they all erupt at once, there is no way people in the northern hemisphere can travel south quick enough to survive on the surface. Only time will tell what happens to us here on Earth."

"Yes, Sir. We'll let you get back to work. Is there any particular day or time when we should call you again?"

"I think it would be best if we contact you once we have a better idea of our progress."

"Yes, Sir. Good luck."

A soft rumble sound got everyone's attention. It only lasted an instant, then Brill stared along the table at Styles. "I thought this place was quake proof?"

"Sir, I didn't make that statement. In my opinion, as long as Yellowstone is erupting, nowhere is completely quake proof."

Brill released a sigh of frustration. "I bet they're not having any in Fort Collins. I knew I should have gone there instead of here. Let's call it a night."

Styles knew telling Brill they would probably be worse in Colorado would serve no purpose. When the president left the room, he brought out his phone and selected his assistant, who answered on the third ring. "Get ahold of the state department and tell them we need a satellite search along the eastern Pacific shoreline for a motorsailer. It's registered to Marcus Hunter, and tell them the president wants it found ASAP."

Chapter 7

WINDANCER:

Vincent was studying the paper charts with Olivia and Rhonda when he heard footsteps behind them. He turned around to see Marcus coming up the stairs, then when Rickie arrived with the radio, he reached out for it. "I was wondering what happened to that."

Rickie did not give it to him. "What's so special about it?"

Vincent exchanged looks with Rhonda before answering. "It is for talking to the Mars colony."

Rickie glanced at Marcus and Olivia before staring at Vincent. "A colony on Mars? You're joking, right?"

Rhonda sat down on a chair before answering. "Over the past three years, we've been sending people and supplies to Mars, and they're at a point where they are self-sustaining. This radio was to be used only if mission control lost contact with them. I thought it would be a good idea to take it with us when we left the ISS."

Olivia moved over to join Marcus and Rickie, then looked at Vincent. "I don't see how having it will help."

"Maybe it will not help, but under the current circumstances, it will not hurt having it around, either."

Geneva suddenly burst through the doorway from outside. "You need to see these pictures my friends are sending me."

Rickie set the radio on the table, then gathered with the others behind Geneva while she showed them the recordings. One from Nebraska showed ash falling like snow. Another showed a picture from space of a one hundred mile wide band of brownish-gray haze, from Montana across North Dakota to the Atlantic Ocean.

The recording changed to show people on the streets and interstate highways walking through the falling ash past stalled vehicles. Another recording showed light ash falling on people smashing store windows and looting, and fighting over bottled water and packaged food.

The recording stopped and Geneva turned it off. "I lost the connection on their end and I haven't been able to get them back."

When Geneva ran out the door, no one spoke for a long moment, until Marcus broke the silence. "And now it begins. How long until we reach Lima?"

Olivia studied the computer monitor. "Three hours."

"I'll be in my cabin. Get me when we get close."

"I will."

When Marcus disappeared down the stairs, Rickie sat on a captain's chair next to her mom and studied Vincent and Rhonda. "What are your plans once we reach Lima?"

Vincent glanced over at Rhonda before answering. "I guess I will take my chances on shore. Would you have a gun or a knife I can have? If you prefer, I will pay for it."

Rickie chuckled at him. "You don't have any money. Even if you did, if things get worse, a few months from now, almost everyone will be dead, and those who survive will use food and water as currency."

Vincent smiled and clasped his palms together under his chin. "It seems God has blessed me again. You seem to have plenty of both. Does that mean you are rich? Because I could enjoy hanging out with rich people."

Rhonda folded her arms across her chest and stared at him. "Stop joking around. We're in serious trouble, Vincent." She turned to look at Olivia. "I'd rather go with you two and Marcus. Wherever that is."

"That's up to my father."

Rhonda lowered her arms and headed for the stairs. "I'll go talk to him before he falls to sleep."

***

Marcus was sitting at his desk, making entries into the log book while pondering his fate in this new environment. When his phone rang from an unknown caller, he let it go to voice mail. A moment later, it rang again with the same number, so he answered. "Who's calling me?"

"If this is Mister Marcus Hunter, I'm calling for professor Richard Styles."

"I'm Marcus. How is the professor these days?"

"He says it's urgent you call him right away. I'm texting you his number. Thank you, Mister Hunter."

Marcus leaned forward while he checked his messages, then touched the blue phone number. It was answered on the third ring and he recognized the man on the face time screen. "Hello, Rich. I understand you want to talk to me."

"Marcus, my friend, I'm really glad we found you. We need your help with the eruptions."

Marcus leaned back in his chair. "How many?"

"Mainly Yellowstone, but several volcanoes around the Pacific are showing activity. From what I've been told, they could erupt at any time."

"I've been out of the loop for three years. Why did you call me?"

"Because you're good at solving impossible problems. The only way to keep the situation from escalating is to relieve the pressure, and I know you'll find a way to do it before it's too late."

Marcus sat straight up in his chair and stared at the screen. "That's impossible!"

"Just think about it and get back to me. No pressure, buddy, but the fate of humanity is on your shoulders."

"Thanks a lot, *buddy*."

The call ended and he leaned back in the chair, then turned to stare out the window at the calm sea, wishing he had not answered the phone. He looked at a dust covered plastic bottle of water in the corner of a small bookshelf, where he had put it when he took possession of the *Windancer* three years ago. That was an interesting story, and he grinned, then his thoughts returned to his friend asking him to do the impossible, creating a sense of self guilt for all those who would die because he didn't have a solution.

His thoughts were interrupted by a knock on his door and he took a moment to regain his composure, then swung the chair around to face it. "Come in."

Rhonda eased the door open and stepped inside, admiring the crown molding around the wood paneled room, before looking at Marcus. "This is beautifully done. Sorry to bother you."

"What's on your mind?"

"I was wondering what your plans are when we get to Lima. More to the point, I really don't want to be dropped off alone in a place where I don't even speak the language. Even worse, if they're a bunch of scared people. I'd rather stay with you and your family on the *Windancer*. Great name, by the way."

Marcus slowly swung his chair around until he was looking out through the window in the stern. "No good deed goes unpunished. I suppose since I rescued you, I'm responsible for you now."

Rhonda moved around to look into his eyes. "That's not what I meant. I'm scared, Marcus, but you're not responsible for what happens to me. All I'm saying is drop me off someplace more secluded. I have survival training, so I'll get by."

"You didn't let me finish. I'm stating a fact. You're a nice lady and I wouldn't do that to you. You're welcome to stay and we'll see how the world ends together."

She smiled. "Thank you. You probably saved my life. Again."

She noticed the dirty plastic water bottle on the bookshelf. "Is that a modern version of a message in a bottle?"

Marcus turned his chair back toward the desk and saw something discolored inside the dusty bottle. He slowly stood and carefully picked it up, then gently wiped the dust away with his hand. He stared inside at a scroll before slowly turning to look over at Rhonda. "This has contained nothing but water for three years. Follow me."

Marcus carried the bottle along the walkway to the inside stairs and up into the pilothouse, where Geneva had joined Olivia, Rickie, and Vincent. "I think it's time we opened the bottle."

Geneva reached out and Marcus let her hold it, then she wiped her thumb over the dust on top of the cap as she stared at the object inside. "Is that a message? What's the story, Marcus?"

"On one of my trips before I had my ship, I was looking for clients of goods to trade. I stopped at a small village and met a man to interpret for me, and we went to the market to see what they had to sell. I was stopped by an old woman selling water from a barrel in a cart pulled by a donkey, but she didn't speak English. Even the interpreter had difficulty understanding what she was saying, but she claimed her water was charmed, and would save those worthy of saving."

Vincent took the bottle and studied the faded label on the plastic. "How did the scroll get inside?"

"That's the strange part. I gave her a twenty-dollar bill, and she emptied the bottle, then poured some of her water from the barrel into it and replaced the cap. I took it back from her and was about to drink it when she stopped me. She scolded the interpreter, who told her to calm down, then he told me what she was saying. Evidently, I must wait and open it at the right moment, or it will not save me. I assured her I would, then she had led the donkey and cart away from the market. It has sat in that same spot on the bookshelf since I got the *Windancer*."

Vincent clasped his hands together around the bottle and looked up at the roof. "Thank you, God, for giving us a sign of your mighty power."

Rickie yanked the bottle from his palms and held it out to Marcus. "I say it's time to open it, Grandpa."

"I agree. Go ahead."

Rickie twisted the cap off and set it on the table, then turned the bottle upside down and caught the scroll as it slid out. She set the bottle down and felt the scroll with her fingertips. "It feels like tanned animal skin, and it's still soft."

She carefully unrolled the thin brown flesh and laid it flat on the chart table, then everyone gathered around her. It showed two sets of symbols along a coastline, and three rivers emptying into nothing. There were a few more symbols and writing next to the outer two rivers, with an X in the center one, then she looked over at Marcus. "Can you read this?"

Marcus leaned closer. "Some of it. It says it's the central coast of Chili, and the names of two of the three rivers."

Olivia compared the coast on the map with the chart of a section of the Chilean coastline, and there were several places where major rivers flowed into the ocean. "This looks like the right area, and there are the two names, but I can't find a third river between them."

Rickie heard beeping from the radar and rushed over to see what it had found, then saw two blips east of their location. The next sweep of the radar showed they were moving fast in their direction and she turned back, where everyone was staring at her. "We've got company."

Marcus grabbed the binoculars and looked east toward the shoreline, three miles away. When he saw the boats, he recognized the design. "Pirates."

Vincent chuckled. "Pirates? You must be joking. We are not in the Caribbean."

Marcus gave him a stern stare. "They're everywhere, Mister Cristallis, and it's only going to get worse."

Marcus moved to the control console and started the engines, then pressed the button to retract the sails. Rickie opened a cabinet to grab six sets of noise dampening headphones and handed them out, while Olivia moved to the corner of the pilothouse and pressed a hidden button. A section of the wood panel slid down, exposing shotguns, rifles, machine guns, and a variety of pistols. She didn't grab any, but stood ready with her headset in one hand.

Vincent accepted the headphones from Rickie. "Are we going to listen to music while we are boarded?"

"No. Put them on."

The low rumble of the *Windancer's* engines was barely noticeable compared to the screaming engines of the approaching boats. When they split up to surround his ship, Marcus set the binoculars down and put on his headset. He made sure his crew had theirs on while the boats were idling a few yards away, with the crews pointing guns in their direction.

When he pressed a button on the control console, the people on the boats immediately dropped their guns to cover their ears as they fell onto the deck, writhing in pain. Marcus waited until all movement from the pirates had stopped, then turned off the ultrasound speakers and removed his headset.

Vincent and Rhonda slowly removed their earphones and stared out the window at the pirate boats bobbing on the surface, then at the bodies on their decks. Rhonda turned and gave Marcus an imploring expression.

Marcus understood her question. "Yeah, they're dead. It was them or us. Help me take their fuel and whatever supplies we can use, then we'll scuttle the boats." He waited until Vincent was looking at him. "Unless you want to take a boat and set out on your own."

Vincent looked into the eyes of the others, then back to Marcus. "Can we expect more pirates?"

"Of course. The world is changing fast, and until all the humans are dead, it's survival of the fittest."

"Then if you do not mind, I would like to stick around."

Marcus looked over at Geneva, who gave him an imploring stare to say no, then he turned back to Vincent. "We'll see how it goes." He looked over at his granddaughter, who frowned and turned away from him.

Rickie went to the gun cabinet and grabbed a semi-automatic, 38 caliber pistol and inserted a clip, then pulled back the slide to insert a round before flipping on the safety. She opened the door to the outside steps down to the main deck, then looked at the others. "Follow me and I'll show you what to do."

Geneva watched everyone head out the door, but she stayed behind and sat on a captain's chair next to Marcus. "That was a neat trick with the ultrasound. What other gadgets do you have built into our ship?"

When she said, '*our ship,*' Marcus looked over at her and smiled. "I have a few more secrets, but for now you should help them. That way you can learn how we operate and where everything is."

"Sure thing. Can't you make Vincent take one of the pirate's boats and leave?"

"We could always shoot him and send him down with them when we scuttle their boats."

"Don't I wish."

When Geneva left the pilothouse, Marcus engaged the propellers and moved the *Windancer* over to the first boat, where Rickie leapt onto the bow and pulled out her gun. Marcus grabbed a rifle and stepped out of the pilothouse, then chambered a round and held it ready for a quick shot if anyone on the other boats was still alive. Olivia instructed the others to wait while Rickie checked the bodies.

Rickie stopped next to the first pirate, but didn't have to check the pulse to know he was dead. The blood coagulating outside all the openings in his head was all she needed to see. She strolled around the deck, looking at each body until she was sure, then leapt back onto the *Windancer*. "We're good to go."

While they dragged a fuel hose across to the boat, Marcus stood watch. He seriously doubted there were any survivors, since the sound system could either kill any human within five hundred feet, or incapacitate up to two thousand feet, depending on the setting.

An hour later, a dozen five gallon containers of fuel for the skiff were stored in a fireproof room. Only a small amount of precious metals and a few jewels on one boat had been worth taking. After strapping the bodies to the gunnels, they sent everything to the bottom of the ocean.

Rickie noticed the handle of a folding knife protruding from the back pocket of Vincent's baggy jeans, and while he was looking the other way, she snatched it out. When he spun around, she looked him in the eyes. "I'll hang on to this for you."

"I will need it if we go ashore."

"No problem."

When Vincent headed out of the pilothouse, Rickie covertly slid the knife into Geneva's hand. "Here's a spare in case you need one."

Geneva slipped it into her front pocket without looking at Rickie. "Thanks."

Chapter 8

NORTHEASTERN COLORADO:

The Atwaters had abandoned the two-lane road and were headed across the open fields toward a mountain range. At the moment, only traces of ash was falling, and they did not need to wear their makeshift cloth masks, but they knew it was only a matter of time before a shift in the wind would bring it their way again. As it was, the landscape had splotches of gray where the ash had drifted into mounds.

Clark was six inches taller than his father, and was first to notice the top of a church steeple. "I think we're headed toward a town."

They continued across the open ground as the partially charred remains of a church appeared in the distance, then burned-out buildings came into view. They slowed their pace as they approached the remains, listening for any sounds to let them know what they might encounter, but the air was deathly quiet.

They emerged onto a paved street through the center of town and strolled past the charred openings that used to be the windows of brick buildings. When they reached the far end of the one-street-town, an arrow on a tourist sign pointed to a silver mine, and they headed in that direction.

Five hundred feet further, the way was blocked by a chain-link fence with a combination lock on the gate. They slid out of their packs and Nancy took a few swallows from a water bottle before studying a map. When she located the town, she used a compass to verify the direction. "We continue heading west for another fifty-four miles. That should put us close to the entrance to the underground facility outside Fort Collins."

Jackson looked at his watch. "It will be totally dark in two hours. There's a concession building on the other side and we should shelter here for the night."

Clark took a sip of water, then studied the fence. "We can easily climb over this. It doesn't even have barbed wire on top."

Jackson had noticed his son still favoring his shoulder, although he tried not to show it. "Let's see if there is another way in."

Nancy checked the gate and realized the lock had been cut and only appeared closed. "There might be someone in there already."

Nancy opened the gate as Clark pulled out his pistol. Jackson brought out his gun, but she kept hers in her backpack. They cautiously went through the opening and past the empty concession stand, then up the steps to the closed steel doors into the mine. Jackson pulled one side open and looked inside, where sunlight coming in through the barred windows illuminated a large room with a diorama in the middle.

Clark moved up beside his father and stared inside. "Hello? Is anyone in there?"

They waited a few moments, but didn't get a reply, then headed out to get their backpacks. Once ready with flashlights, they went to the door and Jackson entered the mine first. He set his pack on the ground, then strolled across the room to a display showing how the work was done with hand tools.

Clark went over to the open gate on a dark tunnel, which descended out of the range of his flashlight. When he turned away, he heard the clatter of approaching footsteps echo from the tunnel. "We have company."

Jackson grabbed his pack from the ground. "Let's get out of here."

Nancy was the first one out through the doorway and stopped until Clark and her father had joined her. She followed them to the backside of the concessions building, where Jackson and Clark cautiously peered around the corner at the mine entrance. She couldn't see and grabbed her father's arm. "Why did we leave?"

"It sounded like there were several of them, and I didn't want us to be trapped inside until we learn who they are. More importantly, what are their intentions?"

"You mean they could be like those religious people we saw?"

"No, those folks were peaceful. I'm worried about the people forming into cults with fanatical leaders. Scared people want to belong to a group, and can be easily influenced to do horrific things to stay in it."

Clark got their attention. "Hey, they're coming out."

A moment later, a young girl strolled out of the entrance, followed by a man, both wearing backpacks and unaware they had company, but they didn't appear armed. Jackson indicated for his kids to stay put, then slowly moved around the corner of the building with his hands slightly raised at his sides. "Hello. My name is Jackson. I was about to check out the mine for some fresh water. Did you find any?"

"I'm Albert. Yeah, in the tunnel. Are you alone?"

"Yes, look, I don't want any trouble. If this is where you're staying, I'll just get some water and leave."

Jackson watched Albert slowly moving his hand toward his backside and he eased his hand down to his own holster. He didn't notice the girl bringing a pistol out from her coat pocket, but caught her movement just as she fired, causing the asphalt in front of him to explode. He raised his hands, glancing into their eyes from one to the other.

Clark and Nancy were listening from behind the concession stand when the gun fired, causing both to flinch and duck back behind the building. Clark peered around the corner and saw his father's hands were raised, but he wasn't shot. He eased back and turned to let Nancy know their father was okay, then saw her staring behind him. When she slowly raised her hands, he spun around and saw a man pointing a shotgun at them, then held his hands up.

The man studied the teenagers for a moment, leering at Nancy. "Both of you join us out front."

When his sister looked up at him, Clark indicated for her to go first, then followed her around the corner. His father still had his hands in the air as they went over to join him, while the man with the shotgun stood behind them.

The girl grinned and kept her gun pointed at the strangers while Albert searched them for weapons, taking Jackson's gun from the holster and finding a pistol in Clark's coat pocket. When Albert stepped back, she indicated for them to lower their arms, then she lowered her weapon and moved closer to the girl. "What's your name?"

"Nancy Atwater."

The girl chuckled. "At-water. It should be Want-water, because the only way you'll get any is if we allow you to have some."

"Okay. What's your name?"

"Feral. How old are you, Nancy?"

Jackson moved in front of his daughter and stared at Feral. "That's none of your concern."

Feral studied Jackson's body from head to crotch, then back to his eyes, before moving over to the boy to do the same. "What's your name?"

"Clark."

"I guess you were a high school senior. Were you a jock?"

"No, just a student. What do you want from us?"

"I'm not sure."

Jackson moved from in front of Nancy and looked at the man behind them, then at Albert before turning to Feral. "Are they your older brothers?"

Feral laughed. "Hell no. I wouldn't have scx with my brother, even if I had one. They're members of a rock band called Head Hunters, and I'm one of their groupies." She looked past him at the man with the shotgun. "What do you think, Simon?"

"I say we keep the girl and kill the men."

Nancy moved between her father and big brother, who tried to shield her. She glanced back at Simon, who was leering at her again, then stared at the ground in front of Feral.

Jackson looked into Feral's eyes. "Please, just take what you want and let us go."

"Where are you going?"

"Nowhere in particular. We're just heading south, hoping to find clean air and water."

Feral stared at Jackson for a moment. "We heard about an underground government facility west of here and that's where we're headed. Do you know how to get there?"

"No, but I heard the same thing."

Simon moved around from behind the prisoners while keeping his shotgun pointed in their direction. "We're wasting time. Let's kill the men and take what's in their backpacks."

Feral studied Jackson and Clark for a moment. "Fine, but don't kill them in plain sight. We don't want to leave a sign we were here."

Simon shoved the barrel of the shotgun against Jackson's chest, while Albert kept his pistol aimed at Clark. "Move over there behind the public bathroom."

Jackson hesitated, staring at Feral. "This isn't right. We didn't do anything to you."

Simon swung his shotgun around, jamming the butt into Jackson's stomach, driving him onto his hands and knees. "Just shut up or I'll shoot you now!"

Nancy jumped between the rifle and her father while staring at Feral. "No! Don't kill them, and I'll go with you without a fight."

Feral folded her arms across her chest as she stared at the girl. "We know they'll come after you. I don't have a choice."

"No, wait! Lock them in the mine. By the time someone finds them, we'll be long gone and they'll never find us."

Clark wasn't about to let his little sister be a sex slave to Simon and ignored Albert's pistol. "Nancy, no!"

When Jackson tried to get up, Simon used his foot to shove him back down. "I still think we should kill them."

Nancy stared up at Feral. "Do we have a deal?"

Feral studied Nancy's body and her seductive stance, while noticing Simon leering at her. "Deal."

"And leave them their packs and supplies. We don't have much, and it's less weight for you to carry."

Simon stared down at her. "You're a demanding little thing, and I like it. Deal."

Nancy knelt next to her father as she and Clark helped him up, then whispered in his ear. "I'll find a way to come back and get you out."

While Feral went to the gate to get the chain, Simon followed Clark and Nancy behind the concession stand and checked Clark and Jackson's backpacks, grabbing most of the food and putting it into his own pack. When he looked at Nancy's pack, there were flowers and toy dinosaurs embroidered all over the outside. He smiled at her, then indicated for them to put the packs on, with Clark grabbing Jackson's before heading around the building to join him.

Jackson took his pack from Clark as Albert indicated for him to head into the mine. He looked over at Nancy with her dinosaur backpack, thinking how young she looked. "Remember, I love you."

"I will, Dad. I guess this is the way the rest of the world will be if the volcanoes keep erupting."

Nancy saw a final nod from her brother before he disappeared into the mine with her father. When Simon slammed the door closed and tied the chain around the handles, she knew there was little chance her family would get out on their own. She turned back toward the town full of deserted, burnt buildings and knew the chance of someone finding them was slim.

She felt a hand on her shoulder and looked up at Simon, leering at her. "What? Do you want to get it out of your system now? If all you want is a quickie, you must not be the stud I heard you are. What was your job in the band?"

Simon was caught off guard by the contradicting statements. "What? I'm a drummer."

"That means you have good rhythm and stamina. I can hardly wait to get you someplace with a bed."

Feral hid her grin from Simon and turned to Albert, speaking loud enough for Simon to hear. "Let's cover some miles before it gets too dark to travel."

Nancy took one last look at the mine entrance, then followed her new acquaintances out through the gate. She knew the fate of her family depended on her, and she was determined to find a way to save them.

Chapter 9

WINDANCER OFF THE NORTHERN COAST OF CHILI:

Marcus, Olivia, and Rickie were in the pilothouse with the bow pointed south, watching the line of boats and small ships coming out of the mouth of the River Rio Lea, which was the first one on the map. Rickie turned around to look at the stern, where Rhonda and Vincent were staring at boats coming out of the harbor, then she studied the charts on the table.

"This third river on the skin map, Quintana, is seventy miles further south. That's a lot of shoreline, with lots of small rivers. Finding the right one is going to be difficult."

"Once we get clear of this traffic, I'll cruse as close to the shoreline as I can, and maybe we'll get lucky."

Rickie draped a shotgun over her shoulder. "I'll be out on the stern to let them know we're armed."

When Rickie headed out the door down to the main deck, Marcus looked over at Olivia, who was grinning at him. "What?"

"She gets that attitude from your genetic side of our family. Just like Geneva."

"I don't know much about genetics, except something about skipping a generation."

"That's true with some diseases, but not genetic traits."

He grinned at her, then looked out the window. "If you say so."

***

Geneva was sitting on the bow and pulled a pack of smokes from her shirt pocket, then counted how many were left. She took one out to light it, but when she realized they were not headed for a city, changed her mind and put it back into the pack.

She put it into her pocket, then got up and strolled along the center walkway between the cargo hatches toward the pilothouse. When she reached the top of the steps and went inside, she looked at the faces of her family before staring out the port side of the ship at the passing shoreline. "Why are we skipping the town?"

Marcus nodded back over his shoulder. "You saw how many boats were coming out of the harbor, but did you notice the ones loaded with supplies? The owners made it apparent they were armed, and I'm sure there was a lot of looting and robberies. I doubt there's anything left worth taking."

She held up her pack of cigarettes. "Do you think we'll find someplace where I can get more of these? This is my last pack."

"I doubt it. Even if we did, I'm sure they'll cost a fortune."

Geneva moved to the chart table and studied the current map of the shoreline, then compared it to their current location. "This is the first river, like on the skin map, so the next one should be the one with the X mark. I'll try to figure out how many miles it is to that next river by using the pointed thing. Let me know if I get it right."

Olivia got out of the captain's chair and moved up beside Geneva at the chart table. "I'll watch."

Geneva used the calipers and the scale to measure the distance to the next river on the new map, then looked over at Olivia. "I must be doing something wrong, because the next major river is Quintana, which is seventy nautical miles away. That seems a lot farther than indicated on the scroll."

Olivia straightened up from leaning over the table. "No, you did it right."

Marcus looked over at them. "On the skin map, only the first and third rivers have names, so the second river might be hidden somehow. Geneva, use your measurement as a scale and do a comparison to find the approximate distance from here to the second river."

Olivia reached out for the calipers. "It's difficult. Let me do it."

Geneva took the calipers out of Olivia's reach and stared at her. "I can do it."

"I'm sorry. I didn't mean you couldn't. I just mean it can be complicated."

Geneva turned away and leaned over the chart table. "Just drop it, okay?"

While Geneva took measurements and wrote numbers on a scratchpad, Olivia gave Marcus a frustrated expression. She was only trying to help.

A moment later, Geneva straightened up from the table. "We should reach the second river in approximately twenty-four miles."

Marcus knew his daughter, and she was about to take the calipers to check the figures. "Good job, Geneva. Twenty-four it is. Olivia, could you get your poor old dad a beer, please?"

Olivia realized what he was doing, since there was beer in the small refrigerator in the pilothouse. "Sure, Dad. Can I get you something, Geneva?"

"No, thanks."

Geneva waited until Olivia went down the inside stairs, then sat in a captain's chair next to Marcus. "She doesn't like me."

"You haven't given her much of a chance to get to know you. Would you mind telling me why?"

"You wouldn't understand."

"I remember when Rickie used to say the same thing when I was raising her. Sometimes she was right. But sometimes she forgot I already raised one young lady through the troublesome teens. It took me a while with Olivia, but I learned. It was easier the second time with Rickie, but every teenager is different. Just know I'm a good listener whenever you need one."

Geneva thought about it for a few long moments, then released a deep sigh of resignation before looking over at him. "Okay. Every time I look at her, it's like seeing my father's face. Sort of. It's hard to explain."

When Geneva turned back to the window, he let the moment hang for a few moments. "Does it make you angry?"

She didn't turn away from the window. "I hated him for leaving all the time! He ruined my life!"

"What about your mother?"

"What about her? She was a slut and a drunk, and didn't care about me. That's all you need to know."

He checked the GPS and speed. If Geneva was correct, they had twelve more miles to go.

Geneva watched a deer bolt into the forest. "I think she did it on purpose to make him mad. He tried not to show it, but he regretted that night in high school more than anything he did in his entire life, and she knew it."

Marcus was glad she was opening up and didn't interrupt. Something he had learned while raising his girls.

Geneva leaned back in her chair and released the lock handle to swing it back and forth while frowning out at the passing shoreline. "I suppose that's why he had to get away, but what I really hated was it meant he regretted creating me that night, too."

"That's not true. He always told me you are the best thing that came out of that relationship. He really did love you with all his heart."

"Whatever. I haven't been able to reach any of my friends, and it sucks. I don't care what the lawyers said, I never should have got on the plane to go live with you."

"Perhaps, but isn't it great being on an adventure with your favorite grandpa?"

"What makes you think you're my favorite?"

"That hurts."

"How come you're so much different from my dad?"

"What do you mean?"

"He was a war hero, and you're just an old drunk."

Marcus stared out across the water. He had thought getting to know each other would help them bond together, but now he wasn't sure. He realized taking her away from a troubled life was what he had decided, not what she had wanted, and she was correct, and now she was stuck out here with him.

Olivia stepped into the pilothouse and sensed the tension in the air, then Marcus turned from the helm and grabbed the beer from her hand. When he headed outside and down the steps without speaking, she moved to the control console and checked the settings, seeing the ship was on autopilot, then she looked at Geneva. "What's going on?"

Geneva got out of the chair. "Nothing."

Olivia turned and watched Geneva head down the inside stairs. When she turned back to the helm, she saw Marcus standing at the bow, sipping his beer.

***

Geneva was sitting outside on the deck with everyone but Marcus, who was in the pilothouse, as they slowly cruised along the shoreline. They had passed her twenty-four mile destination twenty minutes ago, with no sign of the river. Now she wondered if her calculations were wrong.

Marcus stepped out of the pilothouse and looked down at the small crowd on the deck. "We'll keep heading south."

When he heard a beep from the depth sounder, he stepped back inside and saw the digital reading. He continued glancing at the screen as he steered closer to shore, then when the readout slowly changed, he put the propellers in neutral and stepped back outside. "We just passed over a deep channel on the seafloor. It could have been carved out by an underground river."

Geneva looked up at Marcus and shaded her eyes from the setting sun to see him. "We can't see anything through all those weeds and bushes. Maybe that's why no one knows it's there. You can't find it without the map."

Marcus studied the shoreline. "This is the only stretch of beach with thick vegetation instead of sand and desert. Let me get closer using the depth finder. That way we'll have a better idea where to look and we can use our skiff to drive to the edge of the vegetation"

***

Fifteen minutes later, Rickie was driving the skiff propelled by an outboard motor along the edge of the lush foliage, with Vincent helping to search for some sign of a river. Her posture stiffened, then she stood to look over Vincent's head. "I think I see something."

She shut off the motor and moved to the bow, then grabbed a handful of vines and green leafs on the surface. "We've found it! All we need to do is cut away these vines and we can make it through."

Vincent studied the tangled vegetation. "How thick is it?"

Rickie used her hands to spread the foliage apart to see, but could not. "It's at least ten feet, but it's dark, and I can't tell how much farther it goes."

"Ten feet? Are you kidding? It could take weeks to clear a path wide enough and high enough for the boat."

"It's a ship, not a boat, and the vines are not growing from the bottom. They're floating, so it won't be that difficult to hack them in half and push them to the sides. I'll take us back and we'll talk it over with the others."

When they reached the *Windancer*, Rickie tied the skiff off to a deck cleat and they climbed out to join the rest of the crew, then she explained what she knew. "Two people with machetes should be able to cut through in a couple of hours."

Vincent turned from smirking at Geneva to see what the others were thinking, and could tell they agreed with Rickie. "Hold on a minute. That is a lot of work with no guarantee of what we will find on the other side. What if the skin map is a joke and we end up getting stuck in the jungle? You said it yourself, Marcus. Going south is our only chance at surviving."

"And you said the map was a message from God. What are you afraid of?"

Rhonda had an idea and turned to Rickie. "Can we hike along the river bank?"

"It was dark under the foliage, and I couldn't tell. If it's thick, like here at the entrance, we would have to hack our way through."

Marcus saw everyone staring at him. "I agree with Rickie, so we're going through the vines."

Vincent threw his hands in the air in frustration. "I cannot believe this! You are talking Voodoo and witchcraft and that is blasphemous. I wish I had kept one of the pirate boats and I could go my own way."

Geneva glared at him. "I wish you would have kept one, too."

When Rickie hurried down the stairs to the storage lockers, Vincent plopped into one of the chairs. "Fine, but I am not helping."

Geneva raised her hand. "I'll help."

Rhonda admired her enthusiasm. "I could use the exercise."

Rickie came up the stairs holding two machetes in leather cases, then saw Rhonda getting into the skiff. She went to the railing and handed the machetes to her, then turned to Geneva. "I'll work on the vines while you help my mom and Grandpa to get the ship ready to go up the river."

"I'm stronger than you think."

"I know, but you need to continue learning how to operate this ship, just in case something happens to the rest of us."

"What else is there to learn?"

Rickie grinned. "A lot. Trust me."

"When people tell me to trust them, I've learned not to."

"People, yes, I see your point, but we're family. It's different."

"We'll see."

Marcus watched Rickie step down into the skiff and start the outboard motor. When they drove away, he looked at Olivia, Geneva, and Vincent. "Let's lower the masts."

When Vincent didn't get up, Marcus stood in front of him. "You help or you swim."

Vincent looked up at Marcus, ready to challenge him, then he slowly stood from the chair. He looked up at the gray hair and stubble of beard, then into his eyes. "Are you going to throw me over the side?"

Geneva was staring openmouthed at the confrontation when suddenly Marcus's right hand clenched into a fist, then he hit Vincent's nose, driving him backward over the railing into the water. At first she was surprised, then she smiled and hurried over to look down at Vincent, who was floating on his back while holding his nose with one hand.

When Marcus headed up the steps into the pilothouse, Olivia moved up beside Geneva at the railing and saw Vincent appeared to be doing fine. "Come on and help me get the masts down."

"Okay, but they look really heavy."

"Don't worry. The electric winches will do the heavy lifting. We just need to make sure they don't get hung up on anything."

***

In the skiff, Rickie and Rhonda had only hacked through two feet of vines when Rhonda leaned back from the edge and stretched her back out straight. "Five months in zero gravity takes a toll on the human body."

Rickie continued leaning over the bow, hacking at the thick vines, then suddenly stopped. "Hey, come and look at this."

Rhonda moved up beside Rickie and leaned over the bow. "That looks like a cork."

"I know. Help me clear the vines away from it."

Removing the weight of the vegetation allowed the three-foot-long block of black-colored cork to float on the surface, then they noticed some type of rope through the middle. Rickie pulled on the two-inch diameter material and saw there was another block of cork five feet away.

With Rhonda's help, Rickie managed to get a section of the rope exposed on the surface, then scraped away the black slime. "I don't believe it. It's made from braided hair."

"Yes, I see that. I read somewhere that hair takes a long time to disintegrate. This could be as old as the skin map."

Rhonda reached for a machete, ready to hack through the rope, until Rickie grabbed her arm. "What are you doing? If we cut the rope, maybe the vines will part a little easier."

"The woman gave my grandfather the map for a reason, and she meant for him to keep it secret. That meant she didn't want anyone else to find this river. Once we cut it open, anyone can follow us, and they may not be friendly."

"Okay. What should we do?"

"Follow the rope to the nearest river bank."

Ten minutes later, Rickie managed to find the hidden bank of the river, which blended in with the surrounding vegetation, making it invisible. She dove into the water and found the end of the hair rope was looped around a large boulder, eight feet below, then returned to the surface.

Rickie grabbed the side of the skiff next to where Rhonda was standing. "Toss me the end of that yellow rope and I'll attach it to this one."

Rhonda admired Rickie's tenacity as she ripped through the smaller vines and tied the yellow line to the hair rope, then swam back to the skiff. Rhonda looped her section of yellow rope to a cleat near the transom, ready to drag the vines away from the shoreline.

Rickie waited until Rhonda was done. "I need something to pry the rope over a boulder, but I don't want to cut it. Hand me that gaff hook in the brackets beside the driver's seat."

Rhonda snapped the one inch diameter steel and fiberglass rod free, then held it out over the water. "Is this what you wanted?"

Rickie reached up to take the gaff. "Yep."

Rickie gave the thumbs up sign before disappearing below the surface. A few moments later, the vines started moving, floating toward the little boat and the ocean.

Rickie popped up to the surface and grabbed the side of the skiff, then kicked hard to get over the edge. She took over steering and backed them away from the raft of vines and leafs, dragging the mass further from shore.

***

Marcus, Olivia, Geneva, and Vincent watched from the pilothouse as Rickie dragged the mass toward the other riverbank, slowly exposing the open water hidden under a canopy of trees on the other side. Marcus waited until the opening was wide enough to enter, then steered the *Windancer* into the shadow of the trees.

It took only a small amount of throttle for the propellers to overcome the slow flow of the water. When he reached the other side of the mass of vines, he dropped the engines to idle and steered into the current to stay in one place.

Over the radio, they heard Rickie inform them she needed help to secure the rope around the boulder. Olivia looked at Vincent, who ignored the request. She stepped outside and dove into the water, then swam to the bank and waited while the skiff headed her way.

Rhonda took over the skiff and drove through the opening, dragging the mass back in place, and kept tension on the rope while Rickie dove over the side. With Olivia's help underwater, they got the hair rope over the boulder, then the girls bobbed back to the surface.

Once Rickie and Olivia climbed into the skiff, Rhonda brought the throttle down to idle, which released the tension. When the hair rope held, Rickie released the yellow nylon line and hauled it into the boat, while Rhonda drove the skiff to the *Windancer*.

Marcus stood outside the pilothouse, watching Rhonda and Olivia climb out onto the main deck. Rickie tied the bow line of the skiff to the stern, then climbed out and loosened the rope to let it drift a few feet behind the *Windancer*.

Geneva was inside the pilothouse when Vincent strolled in, leering at her. She glared at him as she folded her arms across her chest. "Don't even think about it."

Marcus stepped back inside, then waited until all the ladies joined him in the pilothouse. Once everyone was in the room, he showed them the readings from the depth sounder. "It's thirty-seven feet deep in the middle of the river right here, but it will get shallower the further we go upstream. I brought the centerboard up, and as long as we have at least three feet of water below the keel, we should be okay."

Marcus eased the throttle forward, then the *Windancer* began moving upstream beneath the canopy of limbs and leafs. Narrow shafts of light sparkled on the smooth surface, and bird songs courted them from the river banks as they cruised along at five knots.

Rickie handed Marcus a cold beer. "Well, Grandpa. This is a pretty good adventure."

Marcus grinned and opened the bottle. "I just hope it's worth the trouble."

***

Geneva climbed the steps from the salon onto the deck and continued to the bow, then sat facing forward and lit a cigarette. She was enjoying the serenity of the changing shadows and shafts of light when she noticed Vincent's bare feet suddenly appear next to her. She didn't look up at him. Not even when he knelt beside her.

Vincent stared out over the bow. "I used to smoke. Could I have one of yours?"

"You don't deserve one. Go screw yourself, because you sure as hell aren't screwing me."

Vincent turned to stare at her, receiving a venomous glare, then slowly stood up and walked away. When he reached the deck below the pilothouse, he looked up through the window and saw the rest of the crew staring at him. He sat in a chair with his back to them and stared at the moving canopy overhead.

***

Two hours later, it was nearly dark under the canopy, then the vegetation parted, exposing the darkening sky. Marcus checked the depth and had only six feet of water under the keel, with no idea how shallow it would be up ahead. He looked down at the deck where everyone was gathered, all staring up at the sky, then he stepped outside. "We need to use the skiff to check the depth further upriver, and this is a good place to stop for the night. I'm setting the anchor."

He pressed a button to release the chain, then put the engines in neutral and waited. The ship drifted back with the current for ten feet before the anchor caught and held the ship in place, then he dropped the centerboard into the muddy bottom to keep the ship from swinging in the current. Once it was secure, he shut off the engines and grabbed a beer from the refrigerator, then turned and headed down the inside stairs to the salon to relax.

***

Vincent was on the main deck, sitting in a chair while studying the starboard side shoreline, when he noticed a large pig emerge from a nearly hidden trail through the forest. It stopped and stared at the ship, then he thought the pig was looking directly at him. It sniffed the air, then spun around and headed back into the vegetation.

Vincent stared at the trail for several moments. When the pig did not come back, he looked up at the darkening sky and held his palms together under his chin, then closed his eyes. "Oh, great God of my ancestors. Is this a message?"

He heard pig snorts from somewhere deep in the jungle and opened his eyes to look at the trail. He heard a few more snorts, then he looked up at the sky. "I hope you are not telling me to follow a pig."

The only reply was the chirping of birds in the trees. He lowered his hands and leaned back in the chair, then smelled the aroma of tobacco and smirked to himself. "The pig will have to wait."

Chapter 10

Day 2

NORTHEASTERN COLORADO:

Inside the mine, Jackson and Clark slid their packs to the ground to find their flashlights. Jackson grabbed the door handle for the exit and it turned, then he pushed against the steel. A one inch gap appeared before it stopped moving and he saw the chain on the other side. He jiggled it several times, but it wouldn't budge, and the gap was too small to get his hand through the opening.

Clark circled the room, looking for anything to use as a lever, then grinned as he grabbed a pick from the display. His grin slipped away as he realized the head was made of plaster, and tossed it aside. He aimed his light down the open tunnel, then at a larger tunnel with locked doors he hadn't noticed the last time he looked inside. He moved to the diorama and studied the layout of the mining operation, then grinned as he turned to his dad. "Come over here and look at this."

Jackson moved across the room to the display and stood next to his boy. "What is it?"

Clark pointed to a ventilation shaft. "Both tunnels will take us to this opening and we can get out. If we take the open tunnel, we have to go all the way to the end, but if we can get that second tunnel door open, we'll get there in half the time."

"How do you plan to get that lock open?"

"I'm not. The hinge pins are on the outside of the door. All we need to do is pull them out and the door will fall open."

"Sure, but the diorama showed several side tunnels we need to take to get out. Without a map, we might not remember which ones to take and we don't have any paper to write them on."

"I'll make notes on my arm and we'll keep it short. Look at the first one we take. I'll write 4 on L, 1 on R and so on."

"Okay. Continue making us a map while I find a way to get the hinge pins out."

***

A CANYON IN THE MOUNTAINS:

It was dark by the time Feral let them stop for the night, and Nancy was glad she and Albert were in their own tent, even though she had to put up with Simon in his. She listened to make sure no one had heard her, then turned down the light from the battery-powered lantern to avoid looking at Simon's eyes, now frozen into a permanent stare at the inside top of the tent.

As she slid into her jeans and got onto her knees to zip them closed, she glanced over at his body while putting on her sox and shoes, feeling a chill run up her spine as she thought about what had just happened.

She felt the bruised areas around her throat as she turned her head to study the bruises on her arms, then put on her shirt. He was a mean drunk, and she had no choice. One of them had to die, and it was not going to be her.

She slid into her coat and packed all the food, water, and batteries she could find into her backpack. She saw his gun and grabbed it, then turned off the lantern and slowly unzipped the flap. She crawled partway out and peered at the other tent, then grinned when she heard passionate moaning. She ducked back inside for the lantern, then shoved it into her pack before crawling all the way out.

She stood and slipped the pistol into her coat pocket, then bent over while carrying her pack in front of her as she hurried away. When she felt safe enough to stop, she put the backpack on and tightened the belt to carry the weight on her hips, then grabbed the straps and began jogging through the canyon floor back the way they had come.

***

THE MINE:

Nancy set the lantern on the concrete slab in front of the doors, then began loosening the knotted chain. She dragged it through the handles and hurled it away as she yanked open the door, then grabbed the lantern and smiled as she ran inside. "I'm back!"

Her smile slipped away as she looked around the empty room. The tunnel for the tourists was open, and she headed toward the entrance, then noticed one side of the double doors into the old mine was on the floor. She realized her father and brother had taken that tunnel, but had no idea why.

She hurried to the opening, then cupped her hands around her mouth as she hollered. "Dad! Clark! Can you hear me? If you can, we can leave through the main entrance. I'm headed in your direction. Start heading back and I'll meet you partway."

She waited several moments, then headed into the tunnel, hoping they had heard her and would head back. If not, she knew she had to hurry if she wanted to catch up with them.

Twenty minutes later, the tunnel branched off in three different directions. She stopped and aimed her light at the ground, looking for footprints, but the hard stone was bare. She studied the entrance into the left tunnel, searching for a clue about which way they went. When she didn't see anything, she checked the one on the right, but it had no extra markings.

She continued along the main shaft for what seemed an hour before reaching another branch in the tunnel, then smiled when she saw an arrow from freshly crumbled rock on the floor. She slid her backpack to the ground and grabbed a bottle of water, then took a few swallows while wondering why they had taken this route. She put the bottle away and slipped into her backpack, then quickened her pace along the mineshaft.

***

INSIDE THE MINE:

The beam from Jackson's flashlight finally failed, then Clark turned his light on and they could see where they were going. He aimed his light down the side shaft at a sign warning of old support timbers, and to keep out. He checked the numbers on his arm to make sure it was the correct tunnel, then looked at his father. "This is the way we need to go to get to the ventilation shaft."

Jackson took a drink of water and had an idea. He poured some on one fingertip, then held it up and remained still. "I don't feel any air movement. That shaft might have already collapsed somewhere up ahead, and the ventilation shaft is still a long way from here. We're down to one flashlight and no spare batteries. If we don't head back now, we'll be in the dark before we reach the main chamber, and that's dangerous."

"I think you're right. Okay, I'll lead the way."

***

After being on for most of the night, the light from Nancy's lantern grew dim, and she has to stop to slip out of her backpack to get fresh batteries. With her smaller flashlight on the floor while she changed out the battery in the lantern, the rest of the tunnel appeared black as tar.

She caught a flicker of light in her peripheral vision and turned to look, but it was gone, so she continued working. With the last battery in place, she closed the cover on the lantern and flipped on the switch, filling the mineshaft with bright light. She turned off her flashlight and placed it and the used batteries into her pack, and was putting it on when she heard a voice. She held her breath while her ears strained to hear it again.

***

Clark suddenly stopped walking and aimed his flashlight at the ground. "Hold on a second. I think I see light up ahead."

When he turned off his flashlight, they saw a light reflecting off a wall, three hundred feet ahead where the tunnel curved. "Can you see it?"

"Yes, maybe someone found the mine and opened the door."

Clark turned his flashlight on and headed up the shaft, slowing as he moved around the curve. When his light illuminated Nancy's face, he smiled and ran to her. "I can't believe you came back!"

Nancy set the lantern down and gave him a hug. "It took most of the night to get here."

When Clark and Nancy parted, Jackson wrapped his arms around his little girl. "I hope it wasn't too bad for you."

"Let's not talk about it right now. The main door is open. Let's get out of here."

When Nancy turned around and headed up the tunnel, Jackson smiled as he followed her, with Clark behind him. "I didn't expect to see you so soon."

She glanced back over her shoulder. "Same here. Why did you leave the main entrance?"

"We didn't expect you to come back, and we were heading for a ventilation shaft to get out and find you."

"I guess you didn't find it."

"It was farther than we realized and our batteries were dying, and we had to go back."

"I'm glad you did. I might naught have caught up with you."

Clark stared past his father at Nancy. "That's a nice lantern. Did they give it to you?"

"No, and I'm not sure if they're going to come after me, but we need to get out of here as soon as possible."

"All right. I think we should keep walking in a different direction for a while tonight, then find a decent place to set up camp."

Jackson grinned to himself. "Good idea, son."

Chapter 11

Day 2.

WINDANCER:

The next morning, they were still anchored under the open section of the canopy, and Geneva was on the stern, smoking her last cigarette. She knew her situation was getting worse, and it wasn't just because of her nicotine addiction. Vincent was becoming more aggressive.

Last night, she had been asleep in her cabin when light shining on her eyelids woke her up. She heard the chain for the door lock rattle, but she did not move. She slowly opened her eyes to see Vincent peering into her room through the gap in the doorway. She remained calm as the light through the gap shrank and widened twice, then vanished with the soft click of the door handle latch. She wondered if the others knew what kind of person he was. If not, she knew they wouldn't believe anything she said about him.

She looked out over the water, wondering if Rhonda and Rickie were enjoying their ride in the skiff. They were going upriver checking the depth and direction of the water before they took the *Windancer* upstream, and now she wished she had gone with them. Her posture stiffened when she recognized Vincent's odor as he stopped beside her, but she didn't acknowledge his presence.

Vincent quickly looked around to make sure Marcus and Olivia were still below deck. "Hey, Geneva. Can I bum a smoke?"

Geneva stood and stared into his eyes. She took a long drag on the cigarette before blowing smoke into his face, then tossed the long, unsmoked part of her cigarette into the water. "Nope."

Vincent sneered and grabbed her arm. "Where else do you have a tattoo?"

She yanked her arm free and punched him in the jaw, sending him staggering back against the railing. She pulled out a knife and pressed the button to flip it open, then held it out in front of her as she studied the rage in his eyes.

Vincent rubbed his jaw as he glared at her, and could tell she knew more about using a knife than he did. He turned away and went down the steps to the orange raft floating behind the ship. He climbed in and untied the bow rope, then sat down to grab the ores and rowed to the beach. He got out and dragged it further on shore, then stared across the water at Geneva. When she showed him her middle finger, he turned and headed up the narrow trail his God had showed him.

*****

Rickie was driving the skiff up river, watching the depth finder for any major changes, while Rhonda made notes of the landmarks on a hand-drawn map. An hour ago, they had to increase the power of the skiff as they skirted the starboard side of some rapids, but it would not be a problem for the *Windancer* as long as they kept to that side of the river.

They had traveled under the thinning canopy much faster than the *Windancer* could have, but when they came around a bend, Rickie suddenly slowed the skiff and stopped. Rhonda looked up from the tablet and saw a thirty foot long dock at the bottom bank of the river. "Wow. There must be people living in the area."

"Yeah, let's continue and see if we find any of them."

Rickie increased the throttle and cruised past the dock, then noticed an overgrown pathway at the top of the river bank. "It looks like no one has been here this summer."

Rickie continued taking readings as the canopy became thinner and more spread out, then the river widened to one hundred feet under a clear sky. "We're at three feet deep. I'll cruise to the other side and we'll see if it gets deeper."

The skiff crossed thirty feet of water before it became even shallower. Rickie put the engine in reverse and backed away, then turned the skiff down river. "I'll head back and we'll let them know what we found."

"Wait! Look over there. It's an old rowboat. I wonder why they don't keep it on the dock."

Rickie turned the skiff around and headed back along the shore, until they were next to the side of a small rowboat upside down on the riverbank, then she let the current take them past it on the way downstream. "It looks pretty old. I doubt it still floats."

"If I'm not mistaken, that looks like an old wooden water barrel on the bank above it. I wonder if it's the one the old woman was using."

"That's one tough old lady if she could row all this way from who knows where to here."

Rhonda smirked at her. "Maybe her water really was special."

"My grandpa is gonna love this."

***

Geneva was sitting in a chair on the main deck with Olivia and Marcus, desperately trying to control her urge for a smoke. After her talk with her grandpa yesterday, she had gotten over her anger when she looked at her aunt. Now that they were talking, she found her interesting and easy to be with.

Olivia heard the engine on the skiff getting louder, and looked over at the orange life raft on the beach. When there was no sign of Vincent, she looked over at Marcus. "Someone might have to go search for Vincent before we leave."

Geneva interrupted before he could reply. "We should leave him there."

Olivia looked past Marcus to see her niece. "Why? Because he doesn't help?"

"That, and I don't like the way he looks at me."

"I hadn't noticed."

"He only does it when no one else is looking."

"I'm sorry. I'll talk to him about it."

"And say what? My niece thinks you're a pervert? Don't worry about it. I've been dealing with those kinds of men since I was twelve, and they haven't gotten me yet. I just thought you should know about it."

"Okay. Let me know if things get worse or if there is anything we can do to help."

Olivia stood and moved to the side of the ship as the skiff drifted alongside, then caught the rope tossed by Rhonda and tied it to a deck cleat. Geneva lowered the sling, and once Rickie and Rhonda fastened it to the eyelets of the skiff and climbed out, she engaged the hoist motor and brought it up out of the water. After lowering it onto the storage bracket, she placed the hoist in the weatherproof cabinet.

Olivia smiled and placed her hand on Geneva's shoulder. "Nice job."

Geneva returned her smile, then began latching it down. When she was done, she joined the others in the pilothouse. "The skiff is secure."

Marcus was glad Geneva appeared to be enjoying herself. "Great. Thanks." He looked at Rhonda. "You'd better go tell your friend to get back here or we'll leave him behind."

Rhonda put her hands on her hips. "He's not my friend. I've only known him for fifteen days, and we're not close." She turned to Geneva. "I've noticed the way he looks at you, and I'm sorry." She lowered her hands and gave her a frustrated expression. "Too bad we're decent people or we'd leave him here."

Geneva smirked. "I'm not always decent. I say we leave him with his raft."

Marcus chuckled, then pressed the button to sound the horn twice. "We'll give him ten minutes, then we're leaving. Geneva, let me show you how to raise the centerboard."

"What's a centerboard?"

"Have you seen a sailboat out of the water?"

"Yeah, in a picture."

"The part that hangs down below the water is the keel and keeps a sailboat from sliding sideways. I have one that does the same thing, only I can raise and lower mine, depending on the conditions. On a motorsailer, we call it a centerboard."

"Cool. Show me how it works."

***

THE JUNGLE:

Vincent hadn't realized how far he had hiked from the *Windancer* until he heard two horn blasts from far away. He turned from the large stone statue of a pig squatting on the ground and ran back along the graveled trail, then slid to a stop when it branched off in three directions. He studied each one, searching for his footprints, but found it impossible because of the loose gravel.

He knelt on the ground and clasped his hands together as he stared up at the sky. "My gracious God, show me the path to salvation."

He heard a voice in his head and stood up, then ran as fast as he could along the center trail. After fifteen minutes, he struggled to draw enough air into his lungs and stopped. He thought he heard a horn, but couldn't hold his breath long enough to listen and dropped to his knees. A few moments later, he stopped breathing when he heard the same horn, only much farther away. "Almighty God, don't let them leave me!"

He got to his feet and began jogging back the way he had come, only at a slower pace as he kept muttering. "They won't leave me. They won't leave me."

He brought his hand up to wipe something off his nose, then tried to look at it while jogging, but had to stop to focus on what it was. His sweat melted the tiny gray flake of volcanic ash into a dot on his finger. He continued jogging, but his mind was telling him Marcus would not wait.

***

WINDANCER:

Marcus was in the pilothouse with Geneva, while the others were out on deck, using binoculars to search for Vincent in the jungle on the other side of the beach. The anchor was still holding the *Windancer* in place and Geneva was minding the helm, so he stepped outside.

He caught a small movement in his peripheral vision and turned his head to look. A large pig was standing at the edge of the vegetation, watching them. As he turned back to the river, a small gray flake floated past his face, then another floated down and landed on the railing. When he looked at the others, their attention was still on the jungle. "The ash is falling, and we need to go. Rhonda, I need you up here as my guide."

Marcus stepped back into the pilothouse and took over for Geneva. He engaged the propellers and eased the *Windancer* forward, taking the strain off the anchor chain as he brought it up from the bottom of the river. Rickie was standing on the bow with a hose shooting water to wash the muck off the chain, while he was watching her hand signals to slow down, as it was pulled over the hawser into the chain locker.

Rhonda stepped into the pilothouse and went to the chart table, where she had drawn a copy of her map and landmarks into a large version. As the ship gained speed, she turned around to the rear window and saw Geneva staring behind them. A few moments later, the ship followed a bend in the river and they lost sight of the raft. When Geneva turned around, she was smiling, so Rhonda did the same and gave her a hug.

Marcus felt relieved when he saw Geneva grinning at him over Rhonda's shoulder. When they parted, he got Rhonda's attention. "How far to our first obstacle?"

"Three miles to some rapids, but they're deep enough on the starboard side if we follow my chart."

"Great. Geneva, take over for me while I try to find a radio broadcast of the news."

When Geneva smiled and took over steering the ship, Marcus sat in front of the radio and pressed the button for scan mode for the FM frequencies. After automatically searching the entire bandwidth several times, he switched to AM and pressed scan again. It took three times through all the frequencies before it locked onto a signal. He pressed the hold button, and a voice came from the intercom speaker.

"The ash from the eruption of a small island off the northern coast of Chili is spreading east over the jungle, where experts tell us it will be washed from the sky by the rain. In North America, the earthquakes are increasing in magnitude, with the latest one registering 4.3 in Denver, Colorado."

***

THE JUNGLE:

Tears rolled down Vincent's dirt-smudged face as he staggered from the thick foliage onto the edge of a cliff, then stopped to look down. His shirt and pants were heavy with sweat as he dropped onto his hands and knees. His body lurched from deep sobs for a few moments before he gained control of his emotions, then he used the back of his hand to wipe the drool from his chin and the snot from his nose.

He looked over the edge of the cliff, and there was no way down to the bottom fifty feet below, so he stared up at the tinted sky. "Almighty God, take me."

He stood up and looked over the edge, then more tears ran down his cheeks. He spread his arms out, closed his eyes, then dove off the edge.

***

THE DOCK:

Rickie and Geneva leapt off the deck of the ship onto the wooden beams while Marcus kept the rubber bumpers and the *Windancer* against the side. Rickie went to the bow and caught a line thrown by Olivia, quickly securing it to a piling, then she moved to the stern, where Geneva caught the line thrown by Rhonda before tying it off to another piling.

Marcus shut down the engines and stepped out of the pilothouse to look at the girls. During the ride, no one had spoken about Vincent, apparently feeling guilty for leaving him behind. The flakes were falling intermittently, and they didn't need to wear masks, but this was only the second day, and he was afraid it wouldn't last much longer.

Olivia lowered the gangway over the side onto the beams of the dock before going down to join Rickie and Geneva, then knelt down for a closer look at the wood. "They look old, but seem to be in decent shape. They're probably a special hardwood."

Rickie and Geneva strolled past Olivia up the ramp to the top of the riverbank to check out the surroundings. They stepped off onto a path of large flat stones, which appeared to follow the river up and down stream.

Geneva turned the opposite way and pointed. "Hey, get a load of the view."

Rickie spun around and stared through a gap in the green canopy, then turned and hollered down at the ship. "All of you need to come up here and see this."

Marcus stepped off the ship as Rhonda jumped onto the dock and joined him, then they followed Olivia up the ramp and looked west with the others. The ocean was far away and below them, under a lightly tinted sky, with a glowing red dot on the horizon. No one spoke as they stared into the distance, each contemplating the future and ignoring the occasional gray flake drifting through the overhead leafs.

When Marcus sensed someone beside him, he turned to look and was surprised by a young girl, guessing her age to be around eleven or twelve. There was something familiar about her, then his jaw suddenly dropped in recognition of the old woman who had sold him the water. "Is it you?"

The four women turned around when they heard Marcus and stared at the girl before Olivia spoke. "Dad? Do you know her?"

Marcus slowly nodded he did, as he continued to stare at her. "Are you the woman who sold me the water? You look much, much younger than the last time we met. Is it because of your magic?"

The girl began speaking in broken English, and Olivia recognized the urgency in her voice. She knelt in front of her, noticing her leather pants and shirt didn't have any seams, only leather laces up the fronts. "My name is Olivia. Do you have a name?"

"Nina."

Nina grabbed Marcus's hand and tried to pull him along the path, but Marcus gently pulled her hand free and indicated the *Windancer*. "What about our ship?"

Nina put her hands on her hips and stared at the ground for a moment, then bent over and scooped some fine gravel off the ground and let it fall. She gestured to Rickie, Geneva, and Rhonda before swinging her hand toward the path up the mountain. "Olivia. Marcus. We must go now!"

Marcus grabbed her hand and nodded he understood, then turned to the women. "Let's get our belongings, then break out the tarps and cover everything before we go."

Everyone hurried down the ramp to the dock and climbed onto the *Windancer*, including Nina. With her help, it only took a few minutes to cover the pilot house and decks with brown plastic tarps.

Once everyone else was off the ship, Rickie raised the gangway and stored it below, then leapt over the side onto the dock. Once she had her backpack on, she followed Nina, Geneva, and Rhonda up the ramp, then looked down at her mom and grandpa standing next to the *Windancer*.

Marcus placed his hand on the side of his ship. "I'll be back."

Olivia grabbed her father's hand. "Nina seems to be in a hurry, and she probably knows more than we do, so let's get going."

Marcus indicated for her to lead the way, then followed. When the path turned around a bend in the river, he stopped and looked at the *Windancer* one last time, hoping she would be okay, before quickening his pace to catch up with the ladies.

Chapter 12

THE JUNGLE:

Vincent opened his eyes, staring up at flickering firelight reflecting off a rough stone ceiling, which curved down to the stone floor of a large cave. He saw his hands were tied in front of him with a leather strap and his shoes were missing, but he also realized he was surrounded by two-inch diameter tree limbs, all tied together to make the bars of a tall cage.

He slowly stood up and approached the bars, then noticed a little girl, perhaps twelve years old, with feathers braided into her hair. He thought she was pretty and leered at her for a moment, then grinned. "You're a pretty little thing. Do you speak English?" When she ran from the room, he stared after her. "Hey! Wait!"

He looked around and the place was empty. He pulled on a tree limb, but it didn't bend. His stomach rumbled in hunger, causing him to think about the last meal on the *Windancer*, then he leaned back against the wall and slid to the floor. The last thing he remembered was diving off a cliff, and he wondered if this was hell.

He heard voices approaching and stood up, catching a phrase in broken English as the voices got closer. Suddenly, they were quiet as a middle-aged man stepped into the cave. His appearance caused Vincent to back up against the wall, while staring at the white paint on half the man's face. One side of his head was shaved and tattooed, with bones and feathers braided into the hair on the other side. He was also wearing animal skins crudely sewn together through slits in the hide.

When six little boys and six little girls moved into the cave, Vincent had a sinking feeling in his stomach. They all had bare faces and feathers braided into both sides of their hair, but the unsettling part was that all of them held obsidian tipped spears.

Vincent turned from the kids when the man opened the gate on the cell and motioned for him to come out. He looked at the kids holding the spears, each with an angry scowl on their face, so he hesitated to move. The same young girl he saw earlier snarled and shoved her spear through the bars, jabbing the tip into his left forearm before he could move.

"Owe! Why did you do that?"

When it was apparent the little demon was about to jab him again, he leapt through the opening into the room, watching her scowl turn into an angry frown. When the man headed out through the doorway, Vincent immediately followed him out of the cave into the sunlight.

He wasn't sure which person spoke English, but assumed it was the big man. "Hey! I am bleeding out and I cannot put my hand on the wound."

The man looked back over his shoulder. "You will make it."

"How long have I been here?"

"Not long."

"Who are you?"

"I am Gore, the high priest of Lord Anishia."

"There is only one Lord, and he is my God."

The little demon suddenly banged her spear against Vincent's wound. "That is blasphemy!"

Vincent cringed in pain, and it surprised him she spoke English instead of Devilish, and he decided to keep quiet. He followed the strange man along a trail beneath the thick tangled vines and leafs, grateful the little hellion was leaving him alone.

Fifteen minutes later, and after what felt like hours to his bare feet, he emerged into the center of a small area carved out of the mountain. Stone terraces formed continuous benches across three quarters of the area, filled with people facing an elaborately carved wooden table on an elevated platform.

The man led him down the center walkway, past the cheering crowd, where he found their gleeful expressions disturbing. He looked at the back of Gore's head as they continued to the bottom of the excavation.

When they stopped, Gore turned around to face him, indicating for him to get down on his knees, but Vincent looked past him and up at the table while a knot formed in his throat. He felt something slam into the back of his knees, driving them out from under him. He slammed onto the ground, with the skin on the palms of his hands burning from the tiny punctures caused by the gravel. When tears of pain blurred his vision, he leaned forward and wiped them away with the back of his hands.

His vision cleared and he saw a pair of bare feet with gnarled nails and crooked joins in front of him. He followed them up with his eyes to knobby knees below an animal hide skirt, then up to the naked sagging breasts of a hairless old woman.

He flinched when she suddenly grabbed his hair and yanked it back until he thought his neck would break. He stared into her clouded eyes, which appeared to not be seeing anything at all. He caught movement in his peripheral vision just before fingers smeared a cool paste along both his cheeks.

The woman let go, allowing him to rotate his neck to get the kinks out, then two hands slipped under his arms and hoisted him onto his feet. They dragged him up the ramp to the table, but when he saw dried brown flakes in the grooves of the carvings, he realized his intuition about its purpose was correct, and tried jerking his arms free. "Let go of me!"

He yanked and kicked as they tried hoisting him onto the table, managing to push off with his feet to knock them off balance. Two more men suddenly grabbed his ankles, lifting him off the ground and slamming him down onto his back on the table. His adrenalin kept pumping as he kept fighting until a thick strap cinched tight across his chest and his ankles were restrained.

When his wrists were strapped to the table, he gave up and stared at the tinted sky. "Almighty God, have mercy and save me!"

His head was suddenly grabbed, then his jaw was forced open. He tasted a sweet liquid just before his jaw was released and held closed, but he managed to force some of the liquid between his teeth and through his lips. For a moment, he felt it drool down his cheeks, until his face and mouth became numb.

Gore's face appeared to be moving in slow motion as the hallucinogen took effect, then the face was replaced by a hand holding a shiny obsidian dagger, moving in a circle above his chest. He heard chanting and a cheering crowd, and tried to turn his head to find the source, only to discover he was paralyzed, staring at a collidescope sky.

His body could not move, but the anxiety was real as the dagger stopped, poised high above his chest. When the cheering and chanting abruptly ceased, he desperately wanted to close his eyes, waiting for the dagger to cut out his heart, but they seemed frozen open.

It seemed time stood still, then the black blade moved out of sight. His eyes were suddenly covered, and he thought he was floating on choppy water. When the movement ceased, he tried to move his head without success. There was no sound, and he desperately wanted to see what was going on. His mind cried out for help, but his mouth did not respond to his command.

He suddenly found it odd he remembered the verses about hearing, speaking, and seeing no evil, then heard his mind chuckling. The mental noise faded until his mind went blank as he passed out.

Chapter 13

ANDES MOUNTAINS:

Marcus and the ladies reached a circular area paved with flat stones. Seven identical one-lane stone paths headed in different directions, and Nina was about to lead them along one of them, so he got her attention. "How much further?"

Nina pointed at a snow-capped peak in the distance before pointing to one of the paths. "Tronador. Open."

He turned to his family and friend. "She's talking about the extinct volcano, but we'll never make it that far tonight. This seems like a good place to stop."

He felt Nina pull on his arm and turned to see the urgency in her eyes while she pointed at the path. "Okay, I get it. I guess we're continuing."

Nina led them at a quick pace along a trail winding through the thick jungle, occasionally branching off, but still heading up hill. An hour later, they were walking along the base of a vertical rock wall covered in thick vines. When Nina suddenly turned and passed through the hanging leafs, they followed her into the total darkness of a large tunnel.

Marcus stopped to allow Olivia to remove an L.E.D. flashlight from the side pocket of his backpack. She handed it to him and he turned it on, then aimed the light around a fourteen foot diameter tunnel, and smiled in recognition. "This is an old lava tube."

Nina reached over to Marcus and placed her hand on the flashlight. "No."

Marcus turned it off, allowing bioluminescent algae on the walls and ceiling to illuminate the tunnel. "Incredible. Is it natural?"

Nina pointed behind them at the wall of vines and leafs. "Closed. Safe. Come."

Marcus looked at his wristwatch and it was after 4:00 PM. "We've been walking for three hours and we need a break."

Nina grabbed Marcus's wrist and covered the face of his watch. "Come."

When she began hiking up the steep grade, Marcus let the girls go first, then sighed with weariness and followed. After an hour, he struggled to keep up, and forty minutes later, it was all he could do to lift one shoe ahead of the other.

He stopped and bent over, trying to get more oxygen to his leg muscles, when he heard footsteps echoing along the tunnel. They were getting closer, then he was suddenly surrounded by four men. One removed his backpack and held onto it, two picked him up under his armpits, and one grabbed his legs before carrying him up the tunnel.

Ten minutes later, Marcus was looking up as they came out of the lava tube into a large clearing under an evening sky. The men set him on one of the wooden benches near a large fire pit, then he looked over at Olivia, Rickie, Geneva, and Rhonda, who were removing their backpacks.

He grinned as he looked at Nina and the four men, all staring at him. "I feel like a wimp."

Olivia sat next to her father. "I barely made it, and Rickie and Geneva had to help Rhonda during the last part."

Geneva sat on the other side of her grandfather. "I was getting tired, too. What do you make of that?"

Marcus looked where she pointed and saw light coming from a sixty foot high by two hundred foot wide entrance into the side of the mountain. "Incredible!"

Rhonda was studying the shirtless men, guessing their ages to be mid-twenties. They appeared physically fit, but not overly attractive, and all four had scars all over different parts of their bodies. Then she noticed their brown pants had invisible seams and laces up the front.

Her concentration was broken by the appearance of an older woman, who was strolling out of the massive cave entrance. She watched the woman stop for a moment, staring at them before continuing down a shallow slope to join them. She was wearing a long white dress decorated with colored glass beads and polished stones. It, too, didn't have any seams, only the leather laces partway up the front.

The woman smiled at the visitors. "Hello. I'm Daniela, and my hobby is languages. I hope you did not have too much difficulty getting here. Please follow me and we can become better acquainted."

Marcus, Olivia, and Geneva got up to join Rhonda and Rickie, then Marcus held his hand out to the woman, who didn't accept it. "I'm Marcus Hunter, and this is my daughter, Olivia, and my two granddaughters, Rickie and Geneva. This is our friend, Rhonda. Are you the one who sent the old woman with the scroll map?"

The woman turned around without answering. She entered the cave, and they followed, with Nina and the men carrying their backpacks close behind them. When they reached the top of the small rise through the opening, they all suddenly stopped as the cave opened up into a massive, two hundred foot high, one thousand foot wide cavern.

Marcus closed his open mouth. "Good grief! This is incredible!"

It was illuminated by algae on the ceiling, walls, and floor, which showed the sides had rooms and stairs cut into the solid basalt rock. As his eyes adjusted to the dim light, he realized the cavern was at least three thousand feet to the back wall.

Marcus realized a village occupied the vast stone floor, with light showing in the windows of hundreds of wooden and stone buildings, with some three stories high. Glowing algae lined the walkways and the wide main street, making the entire area seem like a nighttime painting.

Geneva moved up beside Daniela. "I noticed your clothing is white instead of brown, like the men's. Do you wear a different color to show your status?"

Daniela chuckled for a moment. "Of course not. No one is any better than anyone else. This was a gift from my great-great-grandson on my one hundred and twentieth birthday six years ago."

A young man was strolling along the road from inside the cavern and noticed the strangers. He stopped and studied their clothing, then their shoes. "I'm Herbert, a cobbler. Your footwear does not look handcrafted. Who made them?"

Geneva studied the man's leather sandals, then her own rubber soled sports shoes, before looking into his eyes. "A machine. I like yours better."

Herbert bent over for a closer look at Geneva's shoes, then knelt down and placed his hand on the toe of one of them before looking up at her. "Would you mind if I look at the bottom?"

When Herbert looked down at her shoe, Geneva placed a hand on his shoulder for balance as she bent her knee and raised her foot. She felt his hand on her ankle as he gently moved her shoe to study the different sides, then eased her foot back onto the ground and looked up at her. She smiled back and forgot about her hand until he stood, then she let go and stepped back.

Olivia had also studied Herbert's sandals while he had knelt down. They appeared to be made of one piece of leather with no seams, only stitches between the five pads below his toes. A strange thought occurred to her, but she knew the idea was ridicules.

Herbert looked down at his own feet. "Too bad yours are smaller than mine, or I'd trade with you right now. Are you here to stay?"

"I'm not sure."

"I understand. I think we will meet again."

Olivia got his attention. "Excuse me, Herbert, but what animal did you use to make your sandals?"

Herbert's elation from meeting the strangers vanished. "I just work with the skins. I do not harvest them."

Daniela decided to interrupt before the visitors could ask more questions about their clothing. "If you will come this way, we have much more to show you."

Daniela continued a short distance from the entrance to a large open area, with wooden chairs and benches forming concentric circles out from the center. She indicated the chairs around an elevated stone slab, then waved her hand at some onlookers. "Why don't you sit down and we will bring you food and drink?"

They did as asked and sat on the handcrafted chairs, then Marcus studied the beautiful scenes carved into the wood. "This is incredible craftsmanship. The attention to detail is amazing."

"Yes, we have many talented people in our village."

Marcus indicated the cavern. "Did you build all this?"

"Not the wall houses. No one knows who built those, and the technology needed to melt basalt rock so precisely is far beyond our capability."

Geneva smirked at Daniela. "Does your capability include tobacco?"

"Ah, you need the chemicals. We don't have anything with tar or nicotine."

"I thought so."

"We have something else to smoke. Usually it's the artists who enjoy it, but there are others who use it to relax."

Marcus gave Geneva a knowing look, then turned back to Daniela. "All of you appear to live simple lives, and you're stuck out here hundreds of miles from civilization, yet you don't act like primitives. Why is that?"

"Because we are educated."

"I know, but growing, hunting, and tanning hides isn't really a well-rounded education. Do you know about electricity? It's a mysterious power we use."

Daniela chuckled and held her hand up for Marcus to stop. "If you prefer to talk electronics, or physics, or stellar phenomenon, or even genetics, we have people who are knowledgeable in those fields of study. Like I said, I'm a linguist. I know our computer predicted a super eruption would not happen for another two hundred and thirty thousand years. What is unsettling is this is the first time it was wrong."

Rickie looked at the others while comprehending what she heard, then turned to Daniela. "I didn't see that coming. I never would have guessed you would have electricity, much less a computer. Who owns this place?"

"All of us living here."

Rhonda got Daniela's attention. "It was our fault the computer was wrong. We deflected a large asteroid from hitting the planet, but a smaller one got past us and hit the Yellowstone caldera. It didn't cause a super eruption, but it's causing other volcanoes to become active."

Geneva noticed how the wooden seats were worn smooth, with a deep imprint of a human butt. She sat down just as several people, all wearing leather pants, shirts, and sandals, set up small tables in front of them. As those people left, more people entered, setting ceramic bowls of steaming liquid and metal utensils on the tables, along with hand blown glasses. Two more people entered, offering water or a red liquid.

When someone showed him the choice of drink, Marcus looked up at the young boy. "Do you have any beer?" He received a blank stare. "I'll have the red stuff."

After the boy poured some into his glass, Marcus picked it up and sniffed the liquid, smiling at the aroma of alcohol. He took a sip and held the glass up to Daniela. "This is excellent wine."

Geneva took a sip of her grandfather's wine and scrunched up her face at the boy. "I'll take the water."

Rickie hid her smile from Geneva until the boy turned to her and she indicated wine. She looked over at her cousin, who was scooping vegetable soup from her bowl, then tasted her drink, and it was delicious.

Olivia had the wine and took a sip before looking over at Daniela. "This is an amazing place. How long have you lived here?"

"I was born here, as was everyone before us, for thousands of years."

Marcus took a long swallow of wine to empty his glass, then held it out to the boy. "Do you grow your own grapes, or get them from somewhere else?"

The boy smiled as he poured the liquid into the glass. "I am Samuel, a vintner. They grow wild around the valley. The vintage you are drinking is from last year, and I am glad you like it."

Daniela was smiling with pride, but it slowly slipped away. "Now all that will change. That is why we summoned you to help us, Marcus."

Marcus accepted the full glass of wine. "Yeah, that's what I thought. If you plan on using my ship, it can't hold this many people."

"We'll talk about it after you are rested. When you are no longer hungry, Samuel will take you to a place to sleep."

When Daniela stood, so did Marcus. "Thanks for your hospitality."

Olivia looked over at her father's grin as he held the glass out to Samuel for a second refill. She knew it would be up to her to make sure Marcus didn't get into trouble on their first night in a new city.

***

Geneva rolled onto her side on her cot and slung her arm over her ears, trying to block the sound of her grandfather's snoring. When that didn't work, she threw off the blanket and sat up on the edge, looking around the empty room, which was illuminated by the algae.

The snoring suddenly stopped, and she was about to lie back down, when she heard a person chanting. She got up and went to the door, easing it open to determine where the sound was coming from. Their rooms were on the ground floor of a three story structure to one side of the opening of the cavern, with her door facing the exit.

She determined the chanting was coming from somewhere outside and stepped through the doorway onto the path. When her grandfather's snoring resumed, she closed the door and headed for the mouth of the cavern. When she reached the crest looking down at the fire pit, it was out, then she went down to follow the sound.

Moonlight illuminated a wide road on the other side of the fire pit. She followed it until a smaller road branched off, heading downhill. She stopped to listen, but there was no sound at all. Not even insects. She was about to head back when she heard a man's distinctive voice speaking from somewhere further down the lower road, but she didn't understand the language. When the voice stopped, the chanting person's voice continued, and she headed toward the sound.

When flickering flames appeared through the trees, she moved into the surrounding vegetation until she could see into a large clearing with a fire pit in the center. She counted nineteen women sitting in chairs facing an elevated platform, where a naked man was strapped into a plain wooden chair, chanting while staring up at the sky.

A man wearing a loincloth and an ornate head mask approached the person in the chair, who continued chanting. While the masked man gently grabbed the hair and held the man's head back, Geneva noticed the skin over one woman's right temple appeared to glow for an instant before she got up and approached the prisoner. The woman brought out a knife and made a tiny slice through the curated artery on the side of the prisoner's neck, then the man let go, and the woman returned to sit with the others.

The masked man appeared to be staring at the crowd as he spoke a few words in a language she didn't recognize. Apparently, everyone in the audience did, because all those who had their right side facing in her direction had glowing temples for a fraction of a second.

The prisoner's chanting continued for a few moments as blood ran down his chest onto the ground, then the chanting stopped and his head wobbled as the bleeding slowed. When the head fell forward and the bleeding stopped, the woman got up and moved close to the prisoner, checking for a pulse.

When the woman opened the man's eyes, Geneva flinched when she saw they were completely gray. After the woman indicated he was dead, two other women got up and unstrapped the arms and legs, then set the body onto a simple wood stretcher and carried it away.

When all the women began standing, Geneva realized they were leaving. She moved onto the road and began jogging back to the cavern, then when she reached the large fire pit, she stopped to catch her breath and check to see if anyone was following her. When no one appeared, she hurried up the rise into the cavern, then headed for her room.

When she opened the door, the snoring sounded louder than before. She hurried inside and was about to shake her grandfather's shoulder, desperately wanting to tell him what she saw, then realized he would still be too drunk to believe or even understand what she told him. Instead, she grabbed the blanket, pillow, and thin pad off the cot and carried it outside, then entered the ladies' room next door and spread them out on the floor.

She lay down and pulled the blanket over her body, then stared at the soft glow on the ceiling while thinking about what to tell her family. The room seemed quiet, compared to hers, then her eyelids closed as she drifted into deep sleep.

Chapter 14

Day 3

SOUTH OF FORT COLLINS, COLORADO:

The Atwaters were strolling along a street, past the charred remains of a large grocery store and dozens of bodies covered in a thin layer of ash. Nancy suddenly stopped and moved to the side of the road to check out two of the people. When she saw their faces, she returned to join her father and brother. "It's Feral and Albert."

Clark stared at the bodies. "Could you tell how they died?"

"Yes, they were shot in the back."

She looked into her father's questioning eyes. "Simon is dead. When we stopped, they started drinking vodka from a bottle. Later, Simon and I went to his tent, and it turned out he was a mean drunk. When he started choking me, I had no choice, and I killed him."

Clark indicated the two bodies. "What about them?"

"When they didn't come over, I figured I got lucky. When I looked outside, they were in their tent, screwing, and didn't hear the gunshot. I took all his supplies and left."

Jackson studied her solemn expression for a moment. "I'm sorry for the way things turned out for you. I should have made us leave the mine as soon as we realized there were other people there."

"I'm okay, Dad. None of us could have known what type of people they were. It's not your fault. Really, I'm all right."

"Okay. We should reach the facility in about six hours. Let's just hope they're still accepting people."

They headed out of the small roadside town toward the foothills on the horizon. As they continued past the last building, a sign proclaimed they were headed to property owned by the US Government Bureau of Land Management.

***

SIX HOURS LATER:

They were walking along the ash covered dirt road toward a fence stretching across the aired landscape when they approached another body. Blotches of blood stained the gray ash covering the person, making it difficult to determine the sex.

Clark reached the body first, then turned to his family. "It's a guy, and he was shot in the back. If he was murdered, how do we know what we'll find when we reach the facility? You know, Dad. I'm wondering if this is worth the trouble. I mean, we don't have a radio, so we really don't know how bad things are outside the stream of ash, and we may get shot before we get there."

"We're too close to stop now. Besides, we're almost out of water. We don't have a choice."

Nancy moved past Clark and continued walking. "It's not that far. Let's keep going."

They continued side by side for half an hour until they approached the fencing. Coils of razor wire on top and bottom of the chain links stretched away over the hills to their left and right, but as they approached the gap in the fence, they noticed an odd-looking mound of gray.

The closer they got, the more red they saw in the gray snow. They all suddenly stopped when they realized the mound under the ash was human bodies. They moved around the outside of the mound until they were forced to climb on top of the bodies to get through the opening for the missing gate.

Nancy grabbed the tall fence pole for balance, then placed her foot on the first body. She grimaced when her shoe compressed a person's chest and gas hissed from the open mouth. She quickly stepped onto the next dead person, then a third and fourth until she could jump onto the ground on the other side.

Clark went next, leaping from body to body until he jumped down next to Nancy, then they both watched their father quickly move over the mound and onto the ground to join them.

Jackson pointed at where they had disturbed the ash, then knelt down and brushed away the undisturbed layer to expose dozens of empty brass bullet casings. He picked up several of them as he stood and studied the base. "Thirty-eight caliber, nine millimeter, and forty-fives. From the number of rounds in this small area, it must have been one hell of a gunfight."

"State your business here?"

They looked around for the source of the voice, then Nancy noticed a small camera and solar panel on top of the tall pole she used for balance, so she waved at it. "Hello?"

"State your name and passcode."

Jackson moved around to look up at the Camera. "My name is Jackson Atwater, and my passcode is walnut zero, zero, seven."

"Confirmed for you and Nancy. Clark, move closer to the camera so we can see your face better."

Clark did as asked. "How's that?"

"Good. Stand by."

Nancy smiled at her father. "Double oh seven?"

Jackson grinned. "Who could forget James Bond?" He was about to say more when he heard the voice from the speaker.

"Facial recognition confirmed, Doctor Atwater. Remove your packs and get comfortable. A vehicle will arrive at your location in fifteen minutes. We will see you soon."

"Hold on a minute. Are you still there?"

"Yes."

"Are you with the government?"

"Yes. Why do you ask?"

"After everything that's happened over the past three days, we have no idea if we are still supposed to go to the underground facility. I'm not even sure if we are in the correct place."

"Don't worry. You're in the right place. Your ride will be there in fourteen minutes."

Everyone felt a sense of relief they had made it, and smiled at each other. They removed their packs to use as seats so they did not have to sit on the ash, facing away from the bodies at the colorless landscape.

A few minutes later, everyone stood and looked toward the sound of vehicles approaching, which were leaving waves of ash roiling across the ground behind them. The two military vehicles slowed down as they approached the gate to stop churning up the dust, then parked. Four people dressed in military desert camouflage clothing climbed out of the second vehicle, aiming their rifles at the ground, while a very tall soldier climbed out of the passenger side of the first vehicle and approached them.

"Hello, Doctor Atwater. I'm Lieutenant Helen Hershey."

"It's good to finally get here. How many people on the list made it?"

"You're the first."

"How big is the list?"

"Nearly three hundred."

"Well, it's only the third day. What's happening with the eruption?"

"It's still spewing ash, but no big blow. At least, not yet."

"We felt some tremors yesterday and today. Is that because of the volcano?"

"I'm not the one to ask, but we're feeling them here, too. Don't worry. This place was built using reinforced concrete. Grab your packs, but you'll need to give your weapons to my people before you get in. You won't need them while you're here."

The Atwaters did as asked with their packs and weapons, receiving bottles of water in exchange. Once they were seated in the rear seat of the first vehicle, Hershey climbed into the passenger seat next to the driver and they headed across the aired hills.

Clark reached forward and touched Hershey on the shoulder, noticing the red hair tucked under her hat. Even sitting down, she was taller than he was. When she turned around, he pointed behind them. "It looked like a war took place back there."

"That was yesterday, after word got out about this facility. We only have a skeleton crew and had orders to keep all unauthorized personnel out of the facility, but believe it or not, we didn't kill any of them. They were killing each other, hoping to get in. The last person standing was a young woman with a Mohawk haircut and a body covered in tattoos. She tossed a grenade into the last three people fighting over a pistol, but when we refused to let her in, she blew herself up."

Nancy fought hard to hold back her tears. "We saw a lot of fighting on our way here. We even had to kill some people to stay alive."

"I have a feeling if things continue to deteriorate, that will become the new normal."

When Hershey turned back to the front window, Jackson looked ahead as the mountain range appeared to increase in height. Ten minutes later, they drove past two rows of vehicles and stopped at the end, then they climbed out and grabbed their packs. Jackson looked around at the low mountain range, which seemed to form a crescent around the entrance.

They followed Hershey to a concrete wall with a twenty-foot square heavy steel door. Beside it was a four foot by eight-foot metal door, which was next to a thick glass window protecting the security checkpoint. After verifying their faces with recognition software, they heard the buzzer for the door, then Hershey pushed it open.

The Atwaters followed the Lieutenant through the doorway and along a twenty-foot diameter tunnel, then stopped at an oversized door. She opened it enough for them to look inside and indicated the four military people sitting at desks. "The Army has been stationed here since this project began thirty years ago. We have our own facilities up here, but if things get too bad on the surface, we'll join all of you down below. That is, if you ever get down there."

Jackson was noticing the five empty desks while listening to Hershey. "What do you mean?"

"Right now, there are not enough people to open it up for occupancy, so everyone will stay up here until then."

They followed Hershey into the main tunnel, then walked beside her deeper into the mountain. "To the local civilians, this level is a normal military base, with all the normal amenities, like berthing, mess hall, and a rec room. Nothing fancy, but it works for us until we get enough people to open the lower level."

Hershey stopped and went through a set of double doors into the carpeted floors of the living area, looking like the main floor of a barracks. Four people in military uniforms were lounging in part of the recreation area to one side as they stopped to register.

A private rushed over and moved behind the desk, looking slightly embarrassed as he stood at attention in front of the Lieutenant. "I'm sorry, Ma'am. I didn't know we were getting any new people."

"That's okay. At ease, Private Burley. This is the Atwater family, and they'll need living accommodations. Show them around and get them settled into rooms."

"Yes, Ma'am."

Hershey turned to the newcomers. "You'll be able to watch the news and catch up on what's going on in the outside world. I'll see you later."

When Hershey headed out of the room, the Atwaters looked at the private, who was staring after the lieutenant, then Jackson cleared his throat to get his attention. "You said something about some rooms?"

"Oh, uh, yes, Sir. Most of the rooms are empty, but they all have two sets of bunk beds in case you want to share a room."

"Thanks. We could use something to eat."

Burley grabbed a ring of four keys and tags with room numbers on them, then handed it to Jackson. "The mess hall is further down the main tunnel outside, through the next door on the right, but it's closed until dinner at sixteen hundred hours. Right now, we don't have any cooks, so we take turns making the meals."

"How many military personnel are stationed here?"

"There are twelve of us, Sir. This all happened so fast, the rest of the soldiers stationed here never made it back from town to relieve us. There are vending machines in the rec area, with snacks, cold bottled water, and a variety of sodas. Be sure to keep the plastic bottles capped before putting them in the recycle bin. They're sanitized and reused. Your rooms are in the officer's quarters, which are down that left corridor. That's also where the Vice President took over one of the general's bedrooms as an office. None of them made it here, either."

"Okay. Thanks for putting us up in the VIP suite."

Burley gave him a puzzled expression. "Excuse me, Sir?"

"Nothing. Thanks."

"Okay, just fill out these forms and you can be on your way."

***

Nancy left their sparsely furnished room and returned to the recreation area, hoping to talk to the soldiers, but found the room deserted. She went into a small room for the vending machines, studying the different choices of packaged food, when she heard someone humming just outside the door. The humming stopped, then a man with graying hair stepped into the room. "Hello."

"Howdy. You're new here."

She could tell he wasn't in the military. "That's right. I'm Nancy Atwater."

He smiled and held out his hand. "It's nice to meet ya. I'm Emory Oleo. You're kinda young to be a soldier."

"I'm not. I'm a high school student, but I'm here with my dad and brother. My dad's a doctor and we are on the list."

"I'm surprised they thought they were ready. I've been here since they started this project thirty years ago, and the entire complex was based on an asteroid or comet impact, where they had plenty of time to get it operational. The eruption caught everyone by surprise, and there is hardly anyone here."

"Are you an engineer?"

"In a way. I'm the maintenance security officer."

"That sounds important. What's it mean?"

He grinned. "I'm the custodian. I don't do bathrooms or cleanup or any of that stuff. The soldiers take care of that. I oil the gears and wind the clocks to keep things running around here."

"Cool. So, which snack do you recommend?"

"I've always been partial to Twix bars."

"Hey, I like those, too."

She inserted her coins and pressed the button, then the spring rotated and the candy bar slid into the tray. She took it out and broke it in half inside the wrapper, then opened it and took one half before handing the other to Emory. "Cheers."

Emory grinned and accepted the wrapped piece, then pushed it up and bit off a chunk. "Umm. I'm going to miss these. Thanks."

"What do you mean?"

"If everything goes to hell on the surface, what we have is all we'll get for a very long time, if not never again."

"This is only the third day since the eruption, but it seems like weeks." She saw her father standing in the doorway and waved him in. "Hey, Dad. This is Emory."

Jackson didn't enter, but acknowledged the man. "Hello. We need to go, sweetie."

Nancy smiled at her new friend. "I'll see you around, Officer."

When Nancy stepped out of the room, she saw Lieutenant Hershey and Clark. "What's going on?"

Hershey indicated the hallway for the officer's quarters. "Follow me. There's someone who wants to meet you."

The Atwaters followed Hershey past several doors for more bedrooms until they reached the end, where the door had the presidential seal. When they stopped, Clark's jaw dropped for a moment. "Are we going to meet the President of the United States?"

Hershey grinned and opened the door, then indicated for them to enter. "No, the vice president."

They stepped into the room with a large desk, a sofa, four chairs, filing cabinets, and cardboard boxes of files on the floor. A small woman got out of a chair from behind the desk, then Hershey introduced her. "Madam Vice President. These are the Atwaters."

Patricia Winston extended her hand. "You must be Jackson. It's nice to meet you."

"Thank you, Madam Vice President."

"That's too long a name, so call me Ms. Winston." She reached over to the girl. "Hello, Nancy. You'll have to excuse the mess. We're still getting organized." She shook Clark's hand. "It's nice meeting all of you."

Jackson noticed something was missing. "Where are the Secret Service agents?"

"We decided they were unnecessary."

A deep rumble preceded a sudden shaking as everyone lost their balance, grabbing at each other for support until they all toppled to the floor. Square ceiling tiles crashed onto their heads and backs, then the lights went out.

Chapter 15

THE CAVE:

Inside the massive cavern, everything was always illuminated in a soft glow from the ceiling, and it was impossible to tell the time of day without looking at the entrance, but Geneva's stomach was telling her it didn't matter. She got up and noticed the other women were gone, then went into the other room and shook Marcus's shoulder. "Wake up. It's time to pay the price for enjoying all that wine."

Marcus rolled onto his back and laid his arm across his eyes to block the soft light radiating from the ceiling. "Doesn't that damn algae ever turn off? What time is it?"

"Morning, I think, because I'm hungry."

Marcus rolled to a sitting position on the edge of the cot. "Yeah, me, too." He got up and stretched. "Where are the others?"

"Probably already eating."

When they stepped out of their room, a forty-year-old woman was waiting, and Marcus held out his hand to her. "Good Morning. I'm Marcus, and this is Geneva. We sure could use something to eat."

She did not accept his handshake, but smiled. "I know who you are. I'm Sheryl, and I'll be showing you around. Let's start with our garden, where you can enjoy breakfast."

He looked around the massive enclosure. "You have a garden in the cavern?"

"Not at this level. We'll go to the one outside, but we also have one deep underground."

Marcus and Geneva followed Sheryl out through the mouth of the cavern and along the stone road Geneva had taken last night. As they moved past the smaller road headed downhill, she noticed it appeared to continue past the small clearing until vanishing into the thick vegetation.

They entered a large open meadow with fruit trees, vegetable gardens, and dozens of people eating a vegetarian diet. Marcus saw his girls sitting at a table with a few people, but they didn't notice him and Geneva. He looked up at the sky, then over at his host. "We seem to be away from the falling ash."

"It's only temporary, Marcus. If the volcanoes in Indonesia and the northern Andes explode, the ash and dust will block the radiation from the sun over the entire planet, and it will become dark. Our only chance of survival will be underground."

"I was hoping to survive this catastrophe on the surface."

"Both of you take what you like to eat from the garden and enjoy your breakfast. I'll come back in a little while to show you more of our village."

Marcus realized something was missing. "Hey, wait a minute. Do you have any coffee?"

"No, but there are a variety of teas to choose from."

"What about some meat to eat?" He noticed a sudden change in her posture and expression. "Did I say something wrong?"

"No. We cannot support domesticated animals below ground, so we are not allowed to add it to our diet. It has been this way for hundreds of years."

When Sheryl strolled away, Marcus and Geneva made their way over to Olivia, Rickie, and Rhonda, sitting at a table with a bowl of assorted fruit in the middle. They grabbed a few pieces and sat down on the opposite side, next to a young man who studied the tattoo on Geneva's arm.

"Excuse me. I'm Brian, and one of my hobbies is painting. What is the meaning of your art?"

"It means I was stupid, because now it's the first thing people notice about me."

"Actually, the first thing I noticed was your eyes. They are lovely."

Geneva felt her face flush as she grinned. "Oh yeah? So, you're a painter. You mean like on walls and ceilings and stuff?"

"All the walls have already been transformed into landscapes. I use canvas made by the craft people for my art."

Rhonda looked around, then turned to Brian. "It seems you have some very talented people in your village. Does everyone have a job?"

Brian grinned. "No one has a job. We each have things we like to do, and we share with those who like what we make. It's a very pleasurable life."

Geneva scoffed at the idea. "Yeah, right. You don't even have phone reception. Don't you want to know what's trending on social media?"

"There is nothing we can do about what goes on in your universe, so why let it affect our happiness?"

"Because if you listened to the news, you'd know everyone is going to die when more volcanoes erupt in a couple of weeks."

Sheryl approached the table and stopped. "If you're finished, I have something to show you."

The group looked around at each other, then got up, but Brian reached out for Geneva's hand as she stood to follow the crowd. "I'd like to show you my art."

Geneva slowly slid her hand free. "Some other time. Maybe."

Brian stared after Geneva while a young woman moved up beside him. "What do you think of her?"

Alison stared after Geneva and her friends until they moved out of sight. "She must be ignorant. Permanently coloring your skin doesn't make sense."

"I find the artwork interesting, if not a little strange."

"I find your art a little strange, too."

"After listening to her talk about what is happening in her universe, I think I would prefer to take my chances on the surface with these new people. If they'll take me with them."

"I still believe Janis. Our best chance of surviving is underground."

Brian suddenly wished he had not mentioned leaving. "Yes, I suppose you're correct about our survival."

When Alison grinned and strolled away, he felt a sense of relief. He knew one other person who felt the same as he did about leaving, so he left the garden to find him.

***

For Marcus, the descending pathway seemed to go on forever until they finally stopped at a stone wall. He wiped the sweat off his face with the back of his shirtsleeve, then dragged his other arm across his wet hair. "How deep are we?"

"We are only five hundred feet below the surface, but we are going much deeper."

"Don't you worry about this volcano erupting, like the others along the Andes?"

"We noticed a slight rise in the elevation of the magma we use for thermal energy, but we are too far south to be affected by the Yellowstone eruption. That is good, because if the magma chamber below our volcano ever rose to the surface, the flow would cover thousands of square miles of land and ocean in a two thousand foot deep layer of lava."

Marcus suddenly remembered Styles' desire to relieve the pressure building in the volcanoes. "How deep is the pocket?"

"Three miles below sea level."

"Do you know how big it is?"

"Nearly twenty miles in diameter. Why do you ask?"

"I'm a volcanologist, and I'm curious."

"I didn't know. You might be interested in seeing how we use thermal energy for power."

"You bet I would."

Rickie moved in front of a smooth part of the wall and dragged her fingers down the surface. "Is this a door?"

Sheryl placed her right palm on the stone, then it slid to one side and she stepped into a ten-foot square room, with a metal door on the opposite side. She waited until everyone was in before closing the door and moving to the other side of the room, then she touched a small button on the opposite door.

Marcus noticed the feel of the air changing, as was the feel of his hair. The cloth against his skin began feeling different, then it was dry. He reached up and touched his hair, finding it was no longer wet. "What's going on?"

"We lowered the humidity so we can go below."

Sheryl touched a series of numbers on a control pad, then the room was suddenly dropping and gaining speed. There were no lights or numbers inside, and after what seemed to be five minutes, the room slowed to a gentle stop. When the door opened, Sheryl's mouth was the only one not hanging open.

Marcus was looking along a walkway between racks of computers, with tiny flickering lights on both sides, which appeared to go on forever. He closed his mouth without looking away. "I'm impressed."

Olivia moved past the others and went through the doorway, then stopped while looking from left to right at the flickering lights on the front of the racks. She looked up at the solid gray ceiling, then down below the walkway, where more computer lights appeared to continue into a bottomless pit. She felt a hand on her shoulder and turned to look at the other girls, who were trying to see what she was looking at. She moved further along the walkway while the others entered.

Rhonda was the last one in, and after seeing what was below, turned to Sheryl. "I can't even imagine the storage capacity of this system. You don't have any sophisticated technology in your village. Why did you build such an elaborate computer?"

"We did not build it. It has been here for over five hundred thousand years, and we are just the caretakers. I was genetically engineered to be a technician, just as all the others were genetically engineered to perform the other tasks needed to sustain our community."

"Then why is it here?"

"To answer every question a human might ask. No individual has power over us because of ignorance, like those in the lowlands."

Marcus studied the racks of computers. "Every question? What about philosophy?"

"There is documentation of debates from a wide variety of the human species, but since it is only philosophical, there can be no definitive conclusions. Only discussions."

Rhonda thought about it for a moment. "That means you don't believe in God."

"It's just a word people use to express the thoughts in their mind. Some say they receive a message from God, and it helps them keep their sanity. Or insanity, as we've learned repeatedly. We should head back to the surface."

Marcus snapped his head around to look at her. "Wait a minute! You offered to show me your generator system."

"Oh, of course. We will have to go further down."

Sheryl was the last person through the doorway into the elevator and closed it behind her, then entered numbers into the touch pad. Geneva easily remembered the sequence, which seemed natural to her, just like when she was on the streets of Reno.

The room gained speed on the way down, then a few moments later, slowed to a stop. The door opened and Sheryl led the way across a small room to the opposite wall, where a moving diagram showed the magma distribution through giant heat exchangers, which were in large tubes straight down into the liquid magma.

Sheryl indicated one of the control panels to Marcus. "As you can see, our ancestors bored these tubes through solid rock, then inserted the heat exchangers into the tubes. The water is flash boiled into steam, which drives the turbans on the generators."

"Very impressive. How do you keep the magma from bursting through the exchangers and reaching the surface?"

Sheryl moved to a different panel and touched three symbols, then another diagram showed a different part of the system. "Part of the steam is used to pressurize the ceramic containment vessel of the heat exchangers."

"To contain that volume of raw magma would take a lot of pressure."

"Yes, forty thousand pounds per square inch."

"That's an amazing system. Is it all controlled by your computer?"

"Of course. Are you ready to head back?"

"Yes, and thank you for showing it to me."

Sheryl indicated for everyone to get back into the elevator, then closed the door and entered the same code. The room quickly gained speed, then after several minutes, slowed and stopped. She slid the door open and the change in humidity was instantaneous, then she led them up to the main tunnel in the cavern, where a line of people were heading down. "Wait here for a few minutes while I get someone to escort you to a special meeting."

Geneva was the first to notice something strange and got Marcus's attention. "Is it my imagination, or are the people in that line carrying luggage?"

Marcus studied them for a moment. "I think you're right. There's one carrying a string instrument and a large bag."

Geneva left the group and ran to the line of people, following them to a larger tunnel going down at a shallow angle. She moved back along the line until she saw a young girl and walked beside her. "Where is everyone going?"

"To live underground until it's safe to return to the surface."

"Do you have enough supplies for all these people?"

"I don't know. I'm a stone mason."

"Yeah, right."

Geneva studied several people in the line, eliminating obvious artists, until she found a woman with a serious expression and strolled beside her. "Hi. I see there are a lot of you headed down to live underground. Do you have enough supplies to take care of so many people?"

"You must be Geneva. One of the visitors."

"That's right. How did you know? Was it because of my tattoo? Word sure spreads quickly in this place."

"That's because we are all linked to the computer. Everyone is curious about your lives in your universe. Once you start sharing your experiences with us, they will be shared with everyone else. And to answer your question. Yes, having an abundance of electricity allows us to grow and make what we need. We also recycle everything."

"I see. Well, good luck."

***

A short distance away, a handsome man stopped to speak to a woman, who pointed out the visitor named Geneva walking with the others. "What about her?"

"I saw her running away from the ritual last night."

"I see. Thank you for telling me."

When the young stranger moved back to her friends, the man followed her so he could listen to their conversation. He tried not to be obvious by keeping his back to them.

***

Geneva joined her family. "It sounds like they're already set up to live underground, and they're planning on staying below until it's safe to return to the surface. I'll tell you right now, I'm not going to spend part of my life that way."

Marcus studied the line of people passing by. "I'm not a mushroom, and I never should have brought my ship up river."

Rickie folded her arms across her chest. "I thought the map was leading us here for a reason, but I guess not. We should go back before it's too late."

The man moved closer to join them. "Hello. I'm Janis. It's nice to finally meet you."

Geneva was looking at the line of people going underground, but her posture stiffened when she recognized the voice. She slowly turned around, half expecting him to be wearing the mask, but instead, saw a very handsome man. When he looked over into her eyes, she knew he was aware she had been in the clearing last night.

Rhonda smiled at the handsome man in his mid-forties, who was wearing black leather pants and shirt while looking at Marcus. She was about to extend her hand to him when Marcus beat her to it.

Marcus reached out, but Janis did not accept his hand. "It's nice to meet you, too. I'm Marcus Hunter."

"Yes, I know who all of you are. Word gets around quickly."

Marcus noticed his ladies were slightly smitten by the man's good looks. "This is a remarkable facility. It seems everyone has a hobby. What's yours, Janis?"

"I'm a historian, and I come from a long lineage of historians going back thousands of years."

Rhonda smiled as she reached out to shake his hand. "I'm Rhonda, and it's a pleasure to meet you."

Janis maintained eye contact as he gently clasped her fingers in his. He knew the look in her eyes and smiled as he kissed the back of her hand. "The pleasure is all mine."

Geneva desperately wanted to warn Rhonda to stay away from Janis, but knew she would sound like a lunatic if she said anything about last night. Especially since she had not seen his face until now.

Janis knew the three women were single, and repeated the hand kisses with Rickie and Olivia. When he turned to Geneva, she looked away, then he turned back to the group. "I overheard you talking about leaving. Your chances of survival are much better down here with us." He noticed four men trying to get his attention, and he looked at Marcus. "Excuse me for a moment."

Marcus turned to his crew. "Something is going on, and I think we should just continue out of the cavern."

Rhonda could not stop staring at Janis's physically fit body and handsome features. "Would you mind if I ask Janis to come with us?"

Marcus looked over at her. "Yes, I mind. He's hiding something. I can sense it."

Rhonda folded her arms across her chest and turned away from him to stare at Janis, who appeared to be arguing with Daniela. When Daniela left the men and approached her group, Rhonda lowered her arms.

Daniela looked around at the faces of the visitors. "There is disagreement about letting you go. Some are worried you will tell your civilization about us and they will try to take what we have."

Marcus's posture stiffened as he glared at her. "Hey, wait a minute. You tricked me into coming here. Why?"

"We did not trick you, Marcus. It must have been the spiritualist, Nina."

"I don't care who it was, we're getting our gear and leaving."

"I suggest you hurry. The natives found your boat."

"Shit! I gotta get back there!"

"Do not worry. Our sentries will stop them."

Olivia moved to where she could look into Daniela's eyes. "You created warriors?"

"Of course."

Rhonda could not stop thinking about the handsome man. "Is there any chance I can stay here with Janis? I mean, live underground with all of you?"

Geneva's pulse quickened as she grabbed Rhonda's arm. "You can't stay here!"

Rhonda turned to face her young friend, then eased her arm free. "Excuse me? Why not?"

Geneva realized everyone was staring at her, and motioned her away from the others. "Because you don't really know these people enough to spend that much time underground with them."

"I appreciate your concern, but it's my decision, and I think I'll be fine."

"I don't think they're telling us the truth. One of them said everyone is connected to the computer, which no one else mentioned."

Rhonda looked over at Janis talking to the other men, then back to her cousin. "They seem to be okay with it. To be honest, I wouldn't mind having access to all that knowledge."

"There's more."

Geneva was interrupted when Janis returned and joined Daniela, then Rhonda moved over to join them. She knew nothing she said would change Rhonda's mind, so didn't try.

Rhonda looked up into Janis's eyes. "Can I stay?"

Janis exchanged looks with Daniela, then smiled at the visitor. "Normally it would be up to the council to decide, but because of the current situation, and since we are also on the council, I say yes."

Rhonda looked around at her friends. "I really appreciate you saving my life and taking care of me. I hope you have a safe trip, and perhaps we'll meet again when all this is over."

Rickie was first to give Rhonda a hug. "Take care of yourself."

After hugging Olivia, Rhonda reached out to Marcus for a hug while kissing him on the cheek. "Thanks for everything. Stay safe."

Marcus hoped she was making a rational decision, not an emotional one. "You stay safe, too.

Geneva noticed Janis staring at her, and wrapped her arms around Rhonda's neck to whisper in her ear. "Be careful around Janis. He's not who he appears to be."

Rhonda let go and moved back to look into Geneva's eyes, seeing a warning in her expression. "Okay."

When Janis and Daniela began walking away with Rhonda, Marcus stared after her until they disappeared among the buildings, then continued to their rooms. They repacked their backpacks, then hurried out of the cavern.

They entered the massive lava tube and were following the path downhill when they heard the patter of human feet catching up with them, so they stopped. Rickie and Geneva took small flashlights from Marcus and Olivia, then moved back up the path. They each brought out a knife, poised to repel any attacker. The running pursuer suddenly stopped, and Geneva recognized the artist.

Brian slowly approached the visitors. "Hello, again, Geneva. Would you be willing to take me and my friend with you?"

Marcus moved up beside his girls to study the boy. "Who's with you?"

Brian moved out of the way to let the man step into the light. "This is the warrior, Oscar. We do not want to live underground."

Marcus recognized the warrior who had helped him up the tunnel. "Are any more following you?"

"No, they do not know we have left the village."

Marcus turned to his ladies. "What do you think?"

Olivia was first to answer. "We have plenty of food."

The first time Rickie saw Oscar carrying her grandfather in the lava tube, she had thought he looked interesting. "I think we should help them."

When Marcus received a nod of agreement from Geneva, he turned to the new passengers. "Why in hell did you make us hike all the way to the cavern instead of meeting us on the ship?"

Brian moved in front of Marcus to look into his eyes. "We did not know you would be part of our destiny until Nina told us."

"How did that little girl know when to meet us at the dock?"

"She has a gift we do not understand. Not even with the help of the computer."

"All right. Let's get going before you're missed."

Chapter 16

SOUTHERN ARGENTINA:

With his wrists clasped in handcuffs in front of him, Vincent had been following Gore and his little demon along a one lane road for three hours, but it felt like ten to his bare feet. Now he was to the point where he didn't care what the little devil did to him, and plopped down onto the dirt.

The girl suddenly spun around to face him, but he remained on the ground, glaring at her. When she threatened to stab him with her spear, he stared up at Gore. "I'm not used to being barefoot and my feet are worn raw. You should have thought of that before taking me on this long hike. I need shoes, or I will not go any further."

He noticed Gore staring back along the road behind him. When he heard a horse snort, he turned around to look at a cartload of five native people being pulled by a single animal. When Gore made them stop, they did not look happy.

Gore turned to look down at his prisoner's expectant expression. "Get into the cart with the others."

Vincent pushed himself up off the ground and smirked at the little girl as he stood. "One of these days, you will not have a weapon, and I will enjoy ravaging you."

When she snarled at him, he climbed into the cart and squatted down in the only space available between two people. He drew his knees up against his chest and folded his arms over them, then rested his head on his forearms.

***

For nearly an hour, Vincent was rocking with the motion of the ruts in the dirt road, unable to sleep, but grateful for the ride. When the cart suddenly stopped, he lifted his head as the others made room for him to get out the back. He eased himself onto the stone ground and moved to the side of the road, stretching his legs as the cart continued on.

He turned and saw a suspension bridge across the fifty foot wide fracture in the rock, then he walked to the edge of the cliff. As he looked down at the raging water eighty feet below, Gore grabbed his arm, and he spun around to face him. "What's your problem?"

Gore held on to Vincent's arm. "I will not allow you to commit suicide, like on the cliff."

Vincent jerked his arm free of Gore's grasp. "I wasn't going to jump. I just wanted to see how deep it is. Where are we going?"

"To see Lord Anishia."

Vincent glanced back over his shoulder at the girl behind him, then he followed Gore across the bridge. When he looked down over the side into the canyon, the water looked deep. He was tempted to jump over the cable, then realized he would not survive on his own, and continued across.

When Vincent reached the other side, Gore strolled beside him, but didn't speak as they followed the road through the trees. "Thanks for letting me ride in the cart."

When Gore didn't respond, he looked at the ground as they continued along a road paved with flat stones. A few minutes later, they made a sudden sharp turn and stopped at an opening through a ten foot tall stone wall. What made Vincent's heart rate increase were the two stone creatures with horns and wings guarding the entrance.

Vincent passed through onto a large plaza paved with red bricks, then stopped to look around at dozens of people going about their business in the marketplace. "This is amazing. How old is the original city?"

"Wait here."

Vincent waited with the girl, while listening as Gore talked to the leader of more than a dozen children. After a few minutes, he returned, but Vincent didn't move. "I heard you mention a ship. What is going on?"

Gore shoved Vincent toward the market center and walked beside him. "This way. Our Lord God, Anishia, wants to see you in the temple."

"I hope she did not mean the room with the ceremonial table. You know. Where you cut out a person's heart."

Gore smirked down at Vincent. "That was my first choice, but she said no."

When Gore turned away, Vincent heard the girl giggle. "How old is your little demon?"

"Fourteen seasons."

Vincent smirked as he turned his head to look back at her and the spear, then toward their destination. "Why is she mean to me?"

"She doesn't like the way you stare at her, but that may change later tonight."

Vincent suddenly stopped walking. "What do you mean?"

"You will need stamina."

Vincent smirked to himself as they continued through the market, then along a narrow street lined with venders selling their wares. When Gore stopped at a large, ornately carved door, Vincent studied the various scenes depicting demons and gargoyles sacrificing humans. He assumed they were depicting hell and was thankful he was not going to such a place.

As he stepped back, his eyes settled on a thick slab of black wood on the wall beside the door. The words; *All praise our Lord God, Anishia*, were carved into the surface. He felt an insane rage building in his mind as he looked up at Gore. "That is blasphemous!"

Vincent hurried to the sign, determined to take it down and smash it to pieces. He grabbed one edge with both handcuffed hands and yanked with all his strength, but it refused to come free. When Gore slammed him onto the ground, he tried to get up, but the demon held the point of her spear against his throat, and he stopped moving.

The door opened and a tall figure appeared with sunlight behind it, and he could not make out any details. Gore and the demon suddenly dropped onto their knees and bowed their heads at the person, but Vincent placed his hands on the floor, feeling the handcuffs digging into his wrists as he pushed himself up. He stood in front of the person, expecting Gore to insist he kneel, but he and the demon remained on their knees with their heads down.

When the person turned and indicated for him to enter the room, he saw the outline of breasts beneath her flowing shirt. He followed the woman inside, with Gore and the demon right behind him. As the woman moved further into the extravagantly furnished room, sunlight through the windows glistened off the gem-handled dagger at the waist of her pants, and illuminated the colorful tattoos of demonic beings on her neck and arms.

Vincent stopped as she went up a few steps to sit in an ornately carved wooden chair, then crossed her knees as she stared down at him. He turned to look over his shoulder, where Gore and his partner were on their knees, bent over with their heads and palms on the carpeted floor. When he turned back, the woman was still staring at him. He assumed she was Anishia, the false God, and he stared back evenly.

The woman was not used to her servants looking into her eyes. "I am your God, Anishia. What is your name?"

He glared up at her. "I am Vincent Cristallis and you are not a God!"

Anishia leapt out of the chair, grabbing a gem encrusted wooden staff and driving it into Vincent's stomach. "Kneel before your God or die!"

Vincent bent over in pain, but refused to lower his knees as he straightened up and glared at her. "There is only one God, and you are not him!"

Gore raised his head enough to see his God holding the staff over Vincent, who appeared to be defiant of her mighty power. When Anishia indicated for him to rise, Gore leapt up and grabbed Vincent by the handcuffs. "Yes, my Lord?"

"Show him his boat."

Vincent felt a sense of hope his God was getting him out of his situation, and gritted his teeth against the pain in his wrists. "Could I at least get something to wear on my feet?"

When he heard the little demon growl, he instantly regretted asking. He waited for the sting of her spear, but it didn't come. Instead, Gore spun him around and shoved him toward the open doorway. He hurried through, followed by Gore and his partner. Now his biggest concern was his feet lasting long enough to make it to the *Windancer*.

***

The trip took less time than he expected, and Vincent recognized the branching gravel paths and view from the top of the cliff. When he heard the grunting of a pig, he smiled and turned toward the sound, but there was nothing to see, and he looked at Gore. "Did you hear that?"

"I only hear the breeze through the forest. Go down that left trail."

Vincent did as asked, only this time he kept to the side of the path in the softer dirt. When the gravel abruptly ended, he moved out from the vines and loose vegetation onto the middle of the packed dirt as it continued down at a steep angle.

Five minutes later, the path leveled off and he emerged onto the beach where he had seen the pig, then he saw the orange raft, and stopped to look at his captors. "I thought you were taking me to my ship, the *Windancer*."

Gore grinned at his prisoner. "My God told me to let you see your boat. Now I will make sure you can see it for the rest of your life."

Vincent stared into Gore's eyes, not sure of his meaning. When his grin didn't waver, Vincent spun around to grab the raft and drag it into the water, but his way was blocked by dozens of children, each holding a spear. When they suddenly released war yells and rushed toward him, Vincent staggered back and spun around into the tip of the demon's spear.

He cried out in pain, placing his cuffed hands over the wound to his ribs, feeling the warm liquid seeping between his fingers. He screamed when one of the children's spears pushed through his left thigh, yelling again when it was pulled out.

Vincent looked closely at the rage in the little devil's eyes while she used the tip of her spear to rip his pants open in the crotch. He dropped to his knees and his eyes followed her movement, as she quickly bent over and reached down between his knees and he felt a pinch. When she grinned and held his manhood out for him to see, his eyes suddenly went wide as his mouth hung open in a silent scream, then his vision slowly faded to blackness as he passed out.

Chapter 17

CAMP DAVID:

President Brill looked up from the papers on his desk as Grant walked into the room. "What's going on?"

"We lost contact with the underground facility after that last earthquake."

"Have you sent anyone to investigate what happened?"

"No, Sir. There is too much falling ash in that area for vehicles or aircraft to get to them. We're assuming they had a cave in and are trapped inside, or else they would have contacted us using a vehicle radio outside."

"I was told that facility was constructed using one inch steel rebar and could withstand up to an 8.7 magnitude earthquake. That was what? A 4.3?"

"I don't know what to say, Sir. We'll need to look into it when this is over."

"How many authorized people made it?"

"That's where we're fortunate, Sir. Only one civilian family."

"What happened to the rest of the people on the list?"

"Because Yellowstone wasn't a super eruption, most of them didn't think it was that urgent to get there, and didn't even get started. That's why we're lucky. If something happened to the underground facility, the loss of life will be far less than if they all had made it."

"There still may be people alive. Have a team ready to go as soon as the ash stops falling."

"Yes, Sir."

"Is there any word from Styles about his friend, Mister Hunter?"

"Yes, Sir. They located him on his boat in Chile yesterday, but he hasn't heard from him yet."

"How are the people handling the eruption?"

"Surprisingly well. So far, the ash has only affected the northern plains and a section of the eastern states."

"Okay. What about Europe?"

"They are not getting as much ash as expected from Yellowstone, but it's only a matter of time before the volcanoes in Iceland erupt, which will darken the skies over central Europe. More of the volcanoes around the Pacific Rim are showing signs of new activity, and we'll have the same problem if they blow up."

"I hate sitting here with no way to stop it. If we've lost the underground facility in Colorado, where else can the people on the list go to?"

"That's the problem, Sir. We've never planned on having to do everything so fast. Even the Colorado facility cannot open without enough people to run things. They'll just have to shelter in place until we devise another plan."

"Okay. If by some miracle the Colorado facility is still operational, then it's the best option. Do whatever it takes to find out what happened to them."

"Yes, Sir."

As Grant turned to leave, the floor shook, and he grabbed the door frame for balance, then it was over. "They're getting worse, Sir. Perhaps we should move you and your family and staff out of California until this is over."

"To where? Let's face it, Mark. The situation will probably continue to disintegrate, so what's the difference? No, I'll stay here until there is no other choice. That will be all for now."

"Yes, Sir."

When Grant left the room and closed the door, Brill leaned back in his chair and stared at the view through the window. "This is not what I had in mind for my first year in office."

Chapter 18

WINDANCER:

Marcus led his party out through the vines blocking the lava tube, then began moving single file along the trail back to the dock. Large flakes of ash were falling intermittently, but he could tell by the buildup on the surrounding vegetation, it had been falling for a while. He was relieved the sun was still shining, although not as bright, and wondered how much was falling in North America.

When they saw the ship, Oscar sniffed the air, then signaled for Marcus and company to wait while he checked things out. He slid his backpack to the ground and grabbed his spear, holding it at waist level as he slowly approached the dock and the ship. He followed a trail of dry blood on the stone path to the top of the ramp and saw the ship was still secure, but there was dried blood around the bodies of two fellow warriors lying on the dock.

He studied the area without seeing anyone, then signaled for the rest of the crew to approach before going down the ramp to his friends. It was obvious the warriors were dead, with one lying face up; his open eyes clouded and staring at nothing. He knelt beside the second man, face down on the dock, then gently rolled him over and felt his neck for a pulse, but didn't find one.

Olivia hurried down the ramp to Oscar's side, then knelt down to study the cuts and stab wounds on the bodies. "I'm sorry they died protecting our ship."

When Oscar noticed a dead animal on the shore thirty feet downriver, he stood and moved to the bottom of the ramp, then waited until his fellow passengers had come down. "I need to check something."

Oscar hurried up the ramp to the trail and followed the narrow path downriver through the jungle. He suddenly stopped when he saw a human body wearing an animal hide waistcloth, lying face down in the water. Seven more bodies were scattered along both sides of the river, and he was proud his two friends had killed so many and protected the ship.

He hurried back to the ramp, then went down to the people removing the tarps. "It is the body of a warrior of Lord Anishia. She claims to be a God of a fanatical society of natives with barbaric customs, who live on the other side of those low mountains. Nina told us they would come, and we sent Lance and Bishop to stand guard. We should leave before more come to find out what happened to them."

While Olivia, Rickie, and Geneva untied the tarps, Oscar and Brian took them away to shake off the light dusting of ash and a few leaves before folding them up and stacking them on the deck. Once the tarps were off and Geneva had lowered the gangway, Marcus hurried up and strolled around the ship, checking for anything out of place, and finding everything as he had left it.

His final stop was the pilothouse, where he inserted his key, started the engines, then he smiled through the window at the others on the dock. His smile slipped away as he noticed the two strangers. He stepped outside to watch while Oscar and Brian rolled the bodies into the water. "Do you need to have a ceremony for your friends before we go?"

Oscar stared up at Marcus. "No. Those are just shells and will be recycled."

"All right. Why don't you come on board with your gear and sit while we get underway, then we'll show you around."

While the new passengers came up the gangway, Rickie and Geneva leapt over the side of the *Windancer* and untied the mooring lines. Rickie kept tension on the last line around the forward piling while Geneva hurried up the gangway and hauled it onboard.

Geneva stopped at the open section of railing and lowered the ladder for Rickie. As the engines grew louder, she felt the ship move forward against the current while Rickie removed the last rope.

Rickie tossed the line onto the deck, then with a final shove to get the ship clear of the dock, she leapt onto the ladder and climbed up onto the deck. While her cousin stored the ladder and secured the arm across the railing, she ran up the stairs to join Marcus in the pilothouse.

Marcus kept the *Windancer* in the center of the river while Rickie moved up beside him. "Which way?"

"There's no place up ahead deep enough to turn the ship around, so you'll have to do it here."

With twin propellers, Marcus was able to spin the ship around one-hundred-eighty degrees in place, then they headed downriver, keeping the speed slightly faster than the flow to maintain steerage.

With a thin layer of ash coating the tree canopy, less light filtered through, and they were forced to use the ship's electric lights to help see where they were going. Fortunately, they had Rhonda's map as a guide for the turns and shallow areas as they navigated their way toward the ocean.

Olivia joined the two passengers on the main deck. "We only have one vacant cabin, but there is a small place to sleep in the cargo hold. We also have pads for the deck chairs if you want to sleep outside. Follow me and I'll show you around."

Rickie waited until the visitors followed Olivia below, then stepped out of the pilothouse and went down the steps to her cousin, who was stowing the tarps in the lockers on the main deck. "Can you believe how lucky we are?"

Geneva gave her a puzzled stare. "What are you talking about? We'll be lucky to survive."

"I'm talking about having Oscar with us, of course. You've seen his muscles and scars. He's a real man."

Geneva grinned at her. "I'm glad you like his looks, but just wait until you get to know him. Jocks can be assholes."

"What do you think of Brian? He's an artist, and you like art."

"He's cute, but kind of shy."

"Well, you're not. I think you should get to know him."

"I'll get to know both of them, eventually. Just don't push me into a relationship. The only thing guys want is to have sex."

"Of course they do. So do most women. It's just that some people can't control their actions or emotions, giving sex a bad reputation."

Geneva closed the locker door and looked around to make sure no one was listening, then grabbed Rickie's hand as they both sat down. "Because I'm tall for my age, guys started looking at me in a weird way when I was twelve, and one tried to rape me when I was thirteen. I got the tattoo so they would find me ugly and leave me alone, but the idea backfired, and all it did was give them an excuse to approach me. It was a stupid mistake, and now I'm stuck with it."

"I'm sorry you had to deal with it alone."

"Yeah, well. That's life, and sometimes it stinks. I've managed to keep the men off me, so I'll be okay."

They heard footfalls coming up the stairs from below as Olivia appeared and stepped onto the main deck before moving out of the way. Brian was next, who smiled at them before heading toward the bow, but there was no sign of Oscar.

Olivia saw the disappointment in her daughter's expression and moved over to sit in a chair beside her. "He volunteered to stay in the cargo hold and wanted to look around the entire area before deciding where he wants to sleep."

Rickie got up from her chair. "I'd better make sure he's comfortable."

Olivia grinned when Rickie hurried down the stairs, then looked over at Geneva, who smirked at her before putting on her sunglasses and lying back in her chair. She looked up at the window into the pilothouse and saw Marcus, then laid back on her recliner.

Geneva thought she was imagining someone playing music, then it faded away. A moment later, she heard the musical notes get louder before fading away again. She sat up and heard the faint musical tones and turned her head until she identified the source. It was coming from the bow, but she didn't see anyone. She stood up and removed her sunglasses, then saw the top of a person's head above the last hatch cover as the sound drifted in her direction.

She remembered seeing Brian going toward the bow, and as she headed in that direction, heard all the notes Brian was playing on a wooden flute. She sat behind him on a hatch cover, enjoying the melody of the song, which seemed to blend with the scenery. When the song ended, she was disappointed it was over. "That was beautiful."

When he recognized the voice, Brian pushed himself away from the mast and off the deck, then turned around. "Thanks. It seemed appropriate for the scenery."

"That's what I thought, too. Did you write it?"

"Yes, just now."

"An entire song in one attempt?"

"It's just a hobby. What do you like to do in your spare time?"

"Hang out at the mall with my friends."

"What type of activity is that? Do you hang by your hands for exercise?"

"We don't hang by anything. We just sit and talk, and watch people."

"Ah, you study people. My primary genetic structure is to understand technical information and operating systems, although there is not much for me to do. Fortunately, my mother was allowed to crossbreed with a man that understood art, and now those hobbies give me much more interesting ways to occupy my time."

"Hold on a second. What do you mean she was allowed to crossbreed? Are you saying you don't get to have sex without permission?"

Brian chuckled for a moment. "That's a blunt way to say it, but it's not what I'm saying. We can be passionate with whoever wants to reciprocate the emotions, but procreation is strictly regulated. Otherwise, too much genetically engineered knowledge in one person's mind would overwhelm them, and they would not be fully functional in any of those hobbies."

"I didn't understand all of what you said, but I get the meaning."

Brian reached into his satchel and brought out an eight by eleven inch book, then handed it to Geneva. "Those are my artistic endeavors."

Geneva opened the cover and saw a blank page with twelve strange black symbols divided into three rows. "Are those letters?"

"Yes, my name and the date in ancient Latin."

She turned the page and saw a rendition of an ocean shoreline drawn with charcoal. "This is beautiful. It must have taken you many years to become this talented."

"Yes, but I enjoyed every moment of learning how to get it correct."

"Do you have people genetically engineered for everything?"

"Yes."

Geneva flipped to the next page, which was of a large group of naked people in and around a rock pool below a waterfall, only this one was in color. "Your attention to detail is incredible. How long have you been learning?"

"Oh, wow. This may come as a shock, but my first lesson using color was two years ago."

Geneva's jaw dropped open slightly, then she closed it. "You're a fast learner."

"I know. Humans are only limited by the data storage capacity of our minds, and some of us are capable of using a larger percentage of our brains. That's why I wanted to go with you."

Geneva turned another page done in water colors, and the next in acrylics. "These are great."

"Thanks. Will you finally tell me the meaning of your art?"

"All right. The right side snake head is hissing and represents fighting for survival. The frowning left side snake head represents calm and thinking, and the center head with no expression represents the balance between them."

"Very impressive. Did you do the staining yourself?"

"No. It was my design, but I had a professional tattoo my skin."

"I like your color choices, and the theme is also significant to the artwork. Is it to remind you to stay in balance with life?"

"Actually, I thought it would be a warning, but it didn't work like I hoped it would. That's why I said it was a stupid mistake. Can I hear your song again?"

"That one doesn't fit the mood. I'll write a new one."

When Brian grabbed his flute and began playing a soft melody, Geneva leaned back on the hatch cover and grinned as she stared at the view. She felt comfortable sitting beside him and was glad he had joined them.

***

Oscar followed Rickie into the pilothouse and saw Marcus minding the helm. "This is an amazing craft, Mister Hunter."

Marcus glanced over at the warrior. "It sure is. And call me Marcus. Are we the first outsiders to see your society?"

"No. Several hundred years ago, a group of explorers managed to find a few of our people downriver, and we learned they were killing animals as trophies to show their mastery of the universe. Our people made sure they never discovered our home, and they left, believing the area was cursed. That's when we hid the entrance to the river, and have maintained it since then."

"I never would have found it if you hadn't helped me with the clue. Can you tell me how you did it?"

"No. That was Nina."

Rickie leaned back against the chart table. "Not only is he smart, Grandpa, but he is genetically engineered to be a warrior, how to hunt, and how to forage for supplies."

Marcus looked over at Oscar. "I don't understand genetic engineering. How can a gene give you all that information?"

"It doesn't give us the information. It only gives us the ability to learn and retain the information about a specific subject much faster than a normal person. Think of it as devoting fifty percent of our synaptic connections to one subject. The average person can only devote less than a fraction of a percent to a subject, and that's what makes the difference."

"Is that why some people can be geniuses about certain topics?"

"In our society, yes. We understand this is a rare occurrence in your universe."

An idea suddenly occurred to Rickie. "Are those genes passed on to your children?"

"Yes, but to a lesser degree than the parent. Those genes create what we consider hobbies. They are things to occupy our time when our specific expertise is not needed."

"I wish that was true in our society," Rickie continued. "About ten percent of the population has violence genes, and harming others or the need for domineering power are their hobbies. Do you have a violence gene in your society?"

"There is no such gene among our people. I only fight to defend, not to attack. My gene gives me the ability to quickly learn and remember all the martial arts. The rest of my knowledge is for my hobbies that Rickie mentioned."

***

Geneva felt a raindrop hit her arm, then another one hit her head. When Brian stopped playing, she heard more raindrops hitting the hatch covers and got up, then moved her body over Brian as a shield while he put his book and flute into his satchel. When he got up, they both hurried between the hatch covers toward the steps up into the pilothouse.

Chapter 19

THE FACILITY. VP'S BEDROOM:
When the shaking and rumbling stopped, the lights came on and everyone slowly sat up to look around at the toppled filing cabinets and the boxes on the floor. Clark shoved pieces of ceiling tiles off his head as he slowly stood up, then looked up at the fractures in the concrete ceiling. He looked at the others for injuries, but everyone seemed okay, then he reached down to help the VP get up. "That seemed a little extreme. Are you hurt?"

Patricia brushed the dirt and dust off her pants and shirt sleeves. "I'm fine." She noticed the telephone on the floor and went over to pick it up. She held the receiver to her ear, then tapped the button for the security office. When it didn't work, she touched another button, then the rest of them, before hanging up and looking at Hershey. "I can't contact anyone. We need to get to the office and find out how bad things are at the entrance."

Hershey had accepted Clark's hand and was standing, then she opened the door into the corridor and looked toward the front desk. She saw two bleeding soldiers hanging on to each other while staggering and hobbling through the double doors into the rec area from the main tunnel. She turned back to Jackson. "We have wounded."

Jackson hurried past Hershey into the corridor, then out to the two young men sitting down on the chairs. "I'm Jackson, and I'm a doctor. Who is in the worse condition?"

Jackson saw one indicate his left ankle while holding his hand over a bleeding wound in his arm. The other man was holding a tourniquet above a bloody rip through his pants. Jackson brought a knife out from his front pocket, then began slicing through the bloody material around the leg injury. "Just hang tight, soldier. We'll get you patched up. What's your name?"

"Private third class Erik Tremble."

Hershey arrived and studied the second man's arm wound, then turned to Nancy and Clark. "Go to any room with sheets and bring them here to use as bandages." She turned back to the man. "You'll be okay, Private Renner. Are there any more soldiers in the main tunnel?"

"I'm not sure, Ma'am. We passed the Sargent just before the earthquake."

Jackson remained kneeling and moved in front of Renner, then gently checked his ankle, feeling him flinch when he touched the bruised area, then relax as his fingers moved past it. "It's not broken, but it could be fractured. I won't know any more until we get you x-rayed. Where's the infirmary?"

"Near the entrance, Sir."

Clark heard voices coming from out in the main tunnel and ran to the doors to yank them open. Three more bleeding soldiers were stepping over chunks of concrete, boulders, rocks, and gravel, shaken loose from the ceiling. They were approaching the doors with two of them holding a makeshift stretcher supporting a body on top. A long way behind them, it appeared the tunnel leading to the surface had completely collapsed.

He waved them over to the doors. "In here. We have a doctor."

Clark held the doors open as the woman and two men carrying the stretcher with another woman on top moved past him into the rec room. "Set her down over there with the others."

Jackson saw the new people and immediately went to the stretcher they were setting on the floor. "What happened?"

A female Sargent, the oldest of the soldiers, indicated the patient's head. "She was unconscious when we found her under the rocks. I did my best to find any major injuries, but I've only had basic first aid training, and I don't know how good I did."

Jackson was checking the unconscious woman's vital signs while listening, then had to cover the patient's eyes with his hand to check for pupil dilation. "I think she has a mild concussion." He stood up. "What about the rest of you?"

The Sargent looked at her people, Private Sterns, and Private Gustavo, who indicated their cuts and bruises, then at Jackson. "We'll be okay, Sir. We just need some bandages. I'm Sargent Shirley Kellerman."

Jackson watched Nancy and Clark cutting up the sheets, then he looked around at the injured soldiers. "I'm Doctor Jackson Atwater. Are there any medical supplies somewhere on this level?"

Hershey was tying a knot in a piece of cloth around Kellerman's bleeding hand. "No, Mister Atwater. Since we have an infirmary on this level, no one thought another station was necessary."

When Patricia approached the soldiers, they were about to stand up, but she indicated for them to remain seated. "Is there any other way out of the mountain?"

They were all quiet until Kellerman spoke. "No, Ma'am. The tunnel has collapsed in both directions, and the only open area is just outside those doors."

"What about through the lower levels?"

"Yes, but we can't get down there from here. I'm sorry, Ma'am."

Patricia folded her arms across her chest and paced across the small room. "This never should have happened. The president told me this place could withstand a magnitude nine earthquake. I'm from California, and I know that wasn't more than a four point five."

Nancy suddenly remembered the maintenance man and got up from a chair. "Hey, has anyone seen Emory?"

Private Renner looked up at her. "You mean the janitor? Yeah, he was doing something in the supply room."

"Where is it?"

"At the end of the enlisted personnel barracks."

Nancy turned and hurried toward the corridor while stepping over ceiling tiles. She passed several open doors into bunkrooms, then had to step over and around chunks of broken concrete from the ceiling above the tiles. As she approached the closed door at the end, she discovered it was blocked closed by three pieces of concrete and stone.

She climbed up onto the pile and beat a rock against the steel door. "Emory? Are you in there?"

A moment later, she heard rapid pounding from the other side, then Emory's muffled voice. "I hear you. Just hang tight while I get you out."

Nancy climbed down and studied the position of the blocks of concrete, then grabbed the smaller piece on top and rolled it off to the side of the door. The next piece was bigger, and sitting on a smaller chunk of concrete. She shoved her shoulder against it, but it didn't move.

She turned and headed back along the corridor to get help, then had an idea and stopped to look into the first bunkroom. She visually searched for a baseball bat or a hockey stick, or anything to use as a pry bar, but there was nothing that would work. She went to the next room and smiled at the weight set, then hurried inside and slid the weights from the bar onto the floor.

She grabbed the bar and carried it back to the supply room, then leveraged it between the block of rock and the door frame. The first shove moved the stone six inches, then she reset it and shoved again. When it didn't move, she put her back against the bar and her feet against the wall, then groaned as she shoved with all her strength.

She nearly toppled over when the large rock slid out of the way, then she tossed the bar aside and dragged the last chunk of concrete away from the door. She grabbed the knob, turned it, then yanked it open.

Emory smiled and stepped out to wrap his arms around Nancy's shoulders. "You have no idea how glad I am to see you, little lady."

She eased him away. "Oh, I can imagine."

"What's the situation?"

"We're stuck in here."

"We? How many?"

"Twelve, including you. The tunnel outside the barracks is blocked in both directions, and we lost contact with the security office near the entrance. We're all trapped in here with no idea what's going on outside."

"Are they injured?"

"Some are. The VP is with us, so I imagine the president will send help when they learn what happened."

"That could take a while. I know a way out."

"Really? How?"

Emory turned and headed across the room to the storage cabinets against the back wall, then pulled on the back edge of the first one. It slid out of the way, exposing a six by five foot rusted metal door in the concrete wall. "This was part of the original design, but it was abandoned because of instability."

Nancy noticed the deadbolt lock on the door. "Do you know where it goes?"

"You bet. It comes out of the next hill over, about twenty miles from here by road."

"How do you know? Have you been inside?"

"I know because I saw the original drawings and watched them working on it."

"Okay, but did you explore it?"

"Well, no."

"We should go tell the others about it."

***

Jackson wrapped a strip of bed sheet around the tear in the skin of a new soldier's left hand, then tied it closed. When he stood up, he saw Nancy and Emory coming out from the corridor. "I see you found him."

Nancy grinned at her father. "And he knows of a way out."

Emory realized everyone in the room was staring at him. "It's an old tunnel from the original layout, but it's been abandoned for twenty years."

Nancy interrupted him. "He saw the drawing but hasn't been in it. We'll just have to chance it and see where it goes."

Patricia got up from a recliner. "I'll go put on some better shoes and be right back."

When the VP hurried down the corridor to her room, Jackson looked at his patients, then at Nancy and Clark. "I have to stay here and take care of the injured."

Nancy indicated she understood. "We'll get help and get you out as soon as possible."

Hershey moved over near the Atwaters. "I'll go with you."

Sargent Kellerman overheard the Lieutenant and moved closer. "But you're the ranking officer, Ma'am."

"I know, but you're injured, and the Vice President is my responsibility. You're next in command, and I'm ordering you to stay here and watch over our people."

"Yes, Ma'am, but wouldn't it be better to order her to stay here? It could be dangerous in that old section."

Patricia was entering the rec room when she heard the conversation. "Actually, I'm the ranking officer down here, and I'm not staying. I never did like being underground, and this is my excuse to get out of here. Who's coming with me?"

Nancy raised her hand. "Clark and I will help you, but we'll need some basic supplies in case it takes longer than expected. Wait while we go get our backpacks to take with us. We'll be right back."

Hershey stood at attention in front of the VP. "No offense, Ma'am, but you're still my responsibility, so I'm going with you."

Patricia noticed the two men who were not seriously injured were starting to get up. "No, both of you stay here with the Sargent and help Doctor Atwater if he needs it."

Hershey looked at the soldiers. "Do any of you have a backpack we can use?"

Tremble raised his hand. "Room seventeen, but there's nothing in it."

"That's okay. I'll take care of it."

Hershey met Nancy and Clark coming out of the officer's corridor just before she entered the enlisted side. "I'm getting another pack. Meet me in the vending machine room and we'll raid them for what we need."

Nancy and Clark entered the rec room, where the VP appeared anxious to leave while talking to their father, then they headed toward them before going to the machines. They refrained from smiling at the animated hand and arm gestures the VP was making, just as she turned to see them and abruptly stopped.

Patricia thought the kids had strange expressions for an instant before they stopped in front of her and their father, then she looked at Clark. "Are we about ready to go?"

"Almost, Ma'am. We just need to stock up on supplies. We'll be right back."

When Patricia realized which room they were going into, she followed them inside. "Do you think it will take more than a few hours to get out?"

Nancy set her pack down and looked at the VP. "I didn't see the drawings, so I don't know. You'll have to ask Emory."

Patricia spun around and hurried out of the room. When she entered the rec room and didn't see Emory, she went over to Jackson. "Do you know where the janitor went?"

"Yes, he was headed to his bedroom."

"Which one?"

"I don't know."

Patricia spun around and hurried over to the soldiers. "Where is Mister Emory's room?"

Sargent Kellerman raised her hand. "It's the last room in the enlisted corridor, next to the supply room."

Patricia hurried to the corridor just as Hershey was returning with the pack. "Did you see the Janitor?"

"No. Why do you ask?"

"Drop that backpack and come with me."

Hershey did as ordered, then followed the VP at a quick pace to the end of the corridor, where she beat on the last bedroom door. She didn't know what was happening, but knew the VP seemed anxious about something.

When Emory opened the door and saw it was the VP, he nearly dropped the damp towel around his waist, then quickly regained his composure. "Yes?"

Patricia gave Emory a quick appraisal, then looked into his eyes. "How long will it take us to get out of that abandoned tunnel?"

"I don't know."

"What do you mean? You saw the drawings."

"Yes, but I never went inside."

"Well, get dressed, because you're going with us."

"I'm what? No, you don't understand. In case you didn't notice because of my simple attire, I'm not in the best physical shape."

"You're the closest thing we have to a guide, so don't argue. And hurry, because we leave in ten minutes."

When the VP spun around and hurried along the corridor, Emory looked up at the Lieutenant. "You need to tell her I can't go with you."

"She's my superior, and I can't do that. I'm going with her, so I'll watch out for you."

"What about a bribe?"

Hershey chuckled. "For me or the VP?"

"All right. I'll be there in a few minutes."

When the door closed, Hershey stopped grinning and headed back toward the rec room. Seeing Emory nearly naked, she knew he was in better shape than he admitted. She snatched up the backpack on the way, then nodded to everyone as she headed across to the vending machines.

Clark was sitting next to Nancy and his father when Hershey strolled into the machine room, so he got up to speak with her. "We don't have enough money between us to buy more than a couple of candy bars."

Hershey set the pack down, then looked around the room. She grabbed a metal chair by the legs, then swung it around with all her strength. The back rest slammed into the front of one machine, shattering the glass. She swung it again into the next machine, but it bounced off. She saw Clark's offer to try, but grinned and swung it again. The glass shattered, then she set the chair down and smiled at the others. "Who needs money?"

Nancy got up, along with Jackson, who watched while she grabbed packages of beef jerky and assorted chips and candy bars. She looked over at Clark and Hershey, who were doing the same, then felt something hard tap her shoulder. She looked up at her father, who was holding out four bottles of water. She added them to her pack, then got up and waited while Clark and Hershey added bottled water to their packs.

Hershey led the Atwaters into the rec room and saw Emory dressed for hiking. He was standing next to the VP, who had her arms folded over her chest while studying everyone, then she moved over and stood in front of the soldiers. "We'll be back for you as soon as possible."

Sargent Kellerman got up. "Good luck, Ma'am. Are you sure you don't want me to go with you?"

"You're needed here, but thanks for offering."

Once Hershey and the Atwaters joined her, the VP lowered her arms and headed back along the enlisted corridor, with her entourage following behind. She stopped when she reached the storeroom, then indicated for Emory to lead the way.

Emory grabbed his backpack from the ground outside his room and put it on, then looked at the VP. "You realize I'm not going to know much about it."

"Just get on with it."

Emory opened the door and entered the storeroom, then continued across to the row of storage cabinets, where he had dragged one section out of the way. He turned around and everyone was staring at him, so he reached into his pants pocket and brought out a small ring with a single key.

He inserted it into the lock and at first it didn't turn, then he looked over at the group. "It's been twenty years since it's been opened."

He turned back to the door and twisted the key a few times, then it turned one hundred and eighty degrees. He turned the knob, heard the latch click, then pushed the door open. The squeal of rusted hinges caused everyone to flinch, then it was open, and he stopped.

The air escaping from the tunnel had a slightly musty odor, then a slight draft of wind blew past them into the tunnel. Emory turned to his new friends and smiled. "The draft is a good sign there's an opening at the other end. Let's just hope they left the lights hooked up."

Emory stepped into the tunnel, then turned back to the right side of the door. He opened the weatherproof cover, then flipped a light switch. A string of temporary lights spaced fifty feet apart illuminated an eight foot by eight foot square, concreted tunnel, then Emory stepped back out and smiled at everyone. "So far, so good."

Nancy wrapped her arms around her father's neck. "I love you, Dad. We'll be back as soon as we can."

Jackson held his little girl close and kissed her on the cheek. "I love you too, so be careful."

Jackson let go and held his arms out to his boy, then they hugged for a moment and stepped back. "I love you, Son. Be careful and take care of your sister for me."

"I will. I love you too."

Jackson waited on one side of the doorway while Hershey entered the tunnel, followed by Emory and the VP. He smiled one last time as his kids waved and followed them in, then waited in the doorway until they disappeared around a corner. He wiped the tears from his cheeks as he turned and headed back to his patients, hoping it won't be the last time he sees his children alive.

Chapter 20

THE RIVER:

It had stopped raining an hour ago, but the weight of the wet ash was more than some of the tree limbs could take. Now, most of the branches hanging over the water were snapped off or sagging, allowing tinted sunlight to reflect off the water.

On board the *Windancer*, Marcus was in the pilothouse with Geneva, while Olivia, Rickie, Brian, and Oscar were sitting on the hatch covers near the bow, studying the riverbanks. According to the GPS, they should be nearing the area where they had spent the night.

Marcus looked over at Geneva, who was standing in the doorway to the steps down onto the deck. None of them liked the idea, but they all knew if they saw Vincent and he wanted a ride, they would have no choice but to take him back on board.

Marcus steered around a bend in the river and saw the orange life raft on the beach, one hundred feet further along the shoreline, then he put the propellers into reverse to slow down against the current. Evidently, Vincent had not returned, so he let the ship drift with the flowing water.

He looked over at Geneva, who was grinning, but as the angle changed, so did her expression. When he looked at the raft, his jaw dropped open while he stared at a human head, which appeared to be sitting in it. As the ship moved further down river past the raft, he saw the head was still attached to the top of the shoulders, which were protruding above the sand. He looked out through the front window at his passengers, who were now standing to stare at the surreal scene.

Geneva was not sure what she felt about the person buried up to their shoulders. She thought perhaps she should feel sorry for them, but only felt elated there was no sign of Vincent. The dark color of the flesh indicated the person was of African descent, then the sound of the engines disturbed a mass of insects covering the head. As the buzzing cloud rose up, she recognized Vincent and smirked.

When the insects once again covered the face, she saw a row of children holding spears on a cliff above the beach, which had not been visible until the vegetation had collapsed. She also saw a wild pig staring at her.

She waved up at them, but they all turned away and vanished. When she turned to the crew, they were studying a thirty-foot pleasure boat anchored seventy-five feet downriver.

Geneva moved back inside the pilothouse and grabbed the binoculars from Marcus, then studied the boat. "It's way too expensive for the three people driving it. I bet they're pirates, and the owners are at the bottom of the ocean."

Marcus put the propellers into full reverse, but by now they were in full view of the boat. The question was who would shoot first?

***

Brian gave Olivia a pleading expression. "We cannot let them go up to the village! They should not even know about this river."

Olivia knew he was correct. "I'm sorry."

Rickie knew it was her fault. "They must have seen the area where I hacked some vines away and found the rope. Let's get up to the pilothouse."

Rickie led the way along the space between the hatch covers, then up the steps to join Marcus and Geneva. "This is our fault, Grandpa. We can't let them continue upriver."

Olivia had an idea. "Let's talk to them on the radio and tell them the river doesn't go anywhere safe from the ash. We let them know the best chance of surviving is in the ocean."

Geneva got everyone's attention. "Their pirates, so we can't trust them." She looked at Marcus. "Isn't that right, Grandpa?"

Marcus glanced over his shoulder to see everyone staring at him. "She's correct, and they'll probably kill us if we try to get past them."

Rickie pressed the button to open the hidden armory. "We'll be ready."

Marcus indicated for Geneva to move closer, while concentrating on keeping the *Windancer* upriver. "I need your help. Could you take Brian below and keep him safe?"

"I can handle a gun. I'd be more useful up here."

"I know, but he cannot defend himself, and it's up to us."

"All right. But you had better be here when this is over."

Olivia waited until Geneva and their guest were below, then turned to Rickie, Oscar, and Marcus. "We have a problem. We can't use the sonic protection because it will also kill all the animals in a five hundred foot radius. How are you going to handle this?"

"I don't know, but we're not capable of ramming them, either. I'm setting the stern anchor so they'll have to come to us from the bow. Maybe that will give us an advantage."

Marcus pressed a button and heard the rattling chain through the open rear window. Nothing happen, then the anchor snagged something solid, causing the ship to stop in the current. He shut down the engines, then everyone waited in silence.

Rickie was surprised when Oscar suddenly ran out the doorway and down the steps to the main deck, then he grabbed one of the spears as he hurried to the bow and stared at the other craft. She knew he had no idea what a gun was, so she grabbed a pistol, then leapt down the steps to stop him. Before she caught up, he was standing at the bow, holding his spear in the air, while shouting at the people on the boat.

To Oscar, it felt like someone had punched him hard in the right shoulder, spinning him around while jerking his hand off the shaft of the spear. He remained standing, staring in numb silence at the small red hole just below his right clavicle bone, then slowly turned his head back around to face the two men standing on the front deck of the pleasure boat.

Rickie was only ten feet away when she heard the gunshot and saw a bullet hit Oscar's shoulder, but he was still standing. In three giant leaps, she tackled him, driving him face first to the deck. When he rolled over to face her, his eyes were wide in shock.

Splinters of fiberglass from the hatch cover zipped over her head as she heard another gunshot. She squatted onto her calves and knees, then tried dragging Oscar further behind the hatch cover. When she could not get enough leverage, she raised her hips to pull him to safety. Fire erupted in her left butt cheek and she dropped onto the deck, grimacing in pain.

***

In the pilothouse, Olivia watched her daughter get shot, igniting the pure rage only a mother could feel. She grabbed an automatic rifle, then pulled the bolt back to slide a bullet into the barrel. She stepped outside and aimed at the men on the boat, then pulled the trigger. She felt the recoil of her gun as she watched the two men on the bow shudder from the impacting bullets, even though their guns were still firing in her direction.

When they dropped from view, she released the trigger and raised the barrel to the wheelhouse of the pleasure craft. When she pulled the trigger, she felt the recoil of three rounds before a bullet ripped through her right bicep muscle, causing her to fling her rifle into the pilothouse.

When holes erupted in the front windows, Marcus dropped to the deck under the spray of shattering glass. He saw the rifle slide across the floor and grabbed the handle, then eased up to the window ledge. He saw the last pirate in the wheelhouse with one hand on the helm and the other holding a sub-machine gun.

In one smooth motion, Marcus rose above the windowsill, aimed, and fired. He watched the man in the wheelhouse flail from the bullet impacts, but the machine gun in his hand was still firing, and several bullets pierced the fiberglass wall below his window. Marcus felt one of them tear into his left leg, causing him to spin around and topple onto the floor, groaning while writhing in agony.

Olivia got onto her knees and used her good arm to crawl over to her father. Her heart leapt into her throat when she saw the bloody hole through his left thigh. The entrance and exit holes were bleeding and she shoved her good hand onto the wound, then hollered toward the stairs down into the ship. "Geneva! It's over, but we need bandages and the trauma kit! Hurry!"

Geneva knew from experience when there were gunshots, people were always hit, and had the kit in hand, with Brian carrying bandages. She ran up the stairs and saw the small wound on Olivia's arm, then knelt beside her grandfather to assess the damage. She unzipped the trauma bag and brought out an inflatable tourniquet, then wrapped it around Marcus's thigh above her aunt's hand.

Olivia was surprised by Geneva's knowledge of emergency first aid, as she watched her deflate the plastic band with a handheld pump. When her niece indicated she was done, Olivia moved her hand off the wound, and the bleeding had stopped.

Geneva waved Brian closer. "Take over and do what Olivia asks."

When Geneva got up, Marcus grabbed her wrist. "Rickie and Oscar are injured at the bow!"

Geneva saw Olivia trying to get up, then indicated for her to stay. "Take care of Marcus while I go check them out."

***

Rickie was lying on her right side next to Oscar, looking into his eyes. She was holding her left hand against the front of his wounded right shoulder, while he was holding his left hand against the hole in the left cheek of her butt. "If we weren't in so much pain, this might seem romantic."

Geneva knelt down next to her cousin and their guardian. "I heard that."

She looked over at Oscar as she wrapped a bandage around Rickie's butt and hips. "I don't see any serious bleeding from your shoulder wound. Can you stand up?"

Oscar used his left arm to help him stand, then looked down at Rickie. "I have never seen wounds made without weapons. Will we be okay?"

"Yes. Help me up and we can get to the pilothouse."

With Geneva and Oscar's help, Rickie hobbled between the hatch covers and stopped at the bottom of the stairs, where Olivia was on her way down. She wrapped her arms around her mother's waist, holding her close while avoiding the bandage and sling around her right arm. "I'm so glad you're alive! How is Marcus?"

Olivia wrapped her good arm around her daughter's neck and kissed her cheek. "I'm feeling the same about you. I'm okay, but Marcus was shot in the thigh and lost a lot of blood. Brian helped him below to his bed, where he can rest. How bad are you hurt?"

Rickie let go of her mom and balanced on one leg while she looked into her eyes, then smiled. "I need someone to get the bullet out of my ass, but I'll be fine."

Olivia looked at Geneva. "You did great. Thank you."

Geneva wrapped her arm around Rickie's waist to help her walk. "Let's take you down to the galley, then I'll come back up and take over the helm until we decide what to do next."

While Geneva and Oscar helped Rickie, Olivia went back up into the pilothouse to check the information on the computer monitor, and everything appeared normal. When Geneva came up the stairs, she hurried down to the galley to perform surgery on her little girl.

Geneva heard crunching sounds under her shoes as she crossed the room to the helm. She was surprised at the damage to the windows and paneling below the controls. She remained standing as she checked the monitor and all systems were functioning, which surprised her considering the damage.

She grabbed the binoculars off the floor and brushed off a few shards of safety glass, then used them to study the other boat. When she didn't see any movement outside or in the wheelhouse, she set the glasses down on the counter.

She remembered seeing a small vacuum cleaner in a charger under the chart table a few days ago. She checked to see if it was still there and it was, then she pulled it out and began cleaning up the mess on the tables, chairs, counters, and floor.

Once satisfied it was all she could do, she opened the refrigerator to grab a bottle of water. When she saw the bottles of beer, she closed her eyes for a moment as she thought about her grandfather. She had looked into his cabin before heading to the pilothouse, where he was lying on his bed, but his pale skin made him appear dead, so she had left the room.

She grabbed a bottle of water and sat in one of the captain's chairs, then turned on the radio and began scanning the various frequencies. She found one where the announcer was speaking English, but there was some static. She locked it into the programs and continued searching, but couldn't understand the different languages. She pressed number three on the programs, and the English announcer returned.

She listened to the bad news for North America, where they are suffering through earthquakes in the west, and dealing with ash in the central and eastern parts of the continent. Small volcanoes in the eastern Pacific that have been dormant for hundreds of years are now showing signs of activity.

Geneva leaned back in her chair and took a long swallow of water, then stared at the pleasure boat. "I sure could use a smoke right now."

Chapter 21

THE CAVERN:

Rhonda looked down at Janis' smiling face. It had been his idea for her to try out her bed in her own small room by lying down on it. She had done as asked, then she had reached out to take his hand, starting something she had desired since she first saw him.

Janis looked up into her eyes while enjoying the warmth of her body. "That was nice."

"Yes, for me, too. It's been a while, and I was afraid I was out of practice."

He smiled. "I thought you were fantastic."

"I noticed you wear black clothes, Daniela wears white, and everyone else wears tan. Is there a reason?"

"Daniela is a spiritualistic scientist, and I'm a historical scientist."

Rhonda was curious about the differences. "Are you saying you don't believe in God?"

Janis smiled, finding her intriguing. "Do you mean a supreme being? As a historian, I know what people believe to be the word of God is actually the voice of their own mind. Usually they use the word when deciding whether to do good or evil, or begging for the strength to survive devastating destruction, or asking forgiveness. It is how they justify their actions."

"What about heaven and hell?"

"I agree the idea is fine for controlling the morality of unenlightened people."

She grinned. "I'm enlightened enough to know my morality isn't satisfied. Are you ready for another round?"

His smile slipped away. "I wish I had time, but I have a busy schedule."

He gently rolled her off his body, then kissed her before sitting on the edge of the bed to put on his clothes. "Have you given any thought to what you would like to do in our community?"

Rhonda sat up and pulled the sheet over her legs and waist. "I'm a mechanical engineer, so something in that field would be nice."

He stood up and looked down at her. "It's not up to me, but I'll see what I can do for you."

"Thanks. This is a big place. How will I find you?"

"I'm sure we'll see each other again. I'd better get going."

When he turned and opened the door, she expected him to look at her before leaving, but he headed out through the doorway without looking back. She stared after him until the door closed, then saw the used condom on the floor where he had dropped it, and realized he had used her attraction to him to seduce her. For a moment, she was upset with him, then remembered she had been the seductress.

It suddenly occurred to her if Janis told other men about what she had done, she might get a reputation as an easy hookup. "Oh, crap!"

She threw off the bed sheet and got up, then adjusted the intensity of the light from the algae radiating from the ceiling to better inspect her room. It did not have running water, only a wash table with drawers, a chair, and a bed. She went to the table and looked into the small mirror on the hardened mud wall, noticing her hair was tousled, but fortunately, she didn't wear makeup. She poured half the water from a pitcher into a bowl. After wetting a small hand towel, she began washing parts of her body.

***

Now dressed, Rhonda was about to open her heavy wooden door to step out into the passageway when she noticed there was no key for the lock. It only took a moment to search the small room, but the key was missing.

She opened the door and stepped outside into the glow of the radiant light from the algae above her head, where both sides of the large side tunnel were lined with doors like hers for as far as she could see. She looked left, knowing it would take her back to the main throughway, then she turned right and glimpsed a naked man with a towel around his waist. She turned around and memorized the symbols above her door, then closed it and headed in the direction of the nearly naked man.

After passing a dozen doors just like hers, she saw the symbols of a man and a woman on two opposing walls, so she stopped and strolled through the short maze walkway into the woman's side. Most of the looks she received from the seven girls and women were of curiosity as they studied her clothes, but one gave her a scathing stare.

Three of them were topless, with the larger endowed women wearing padded leather support bras. She was not going topless, and kept her shirt on as she brought out her comb and looked into the mirror. Once satisfied her hair was good enough, she left the room into the tunnel and continued to find out what's at the other end.

It brought her out to the main thruway, which was a massive lava tube with many side branches. Before she entered the main tube, she looked at the overhead symbols, hoping they were directions, but she didn't understand the language and had no idea where to go. She memorized the symbol above her tunnel so she could find her way back, then entered the main thruway.

Just like her room, the areas were divided by mud or wood-pole walls, from floor to ceiling. Most of them had tanned leather hides stretched across a wooden frame as doors. Some were open, allowing her to see various crafts in different stages of development. As she continued along, the faint notes from a string instrument were barely discernable over the intermittent beating of a hammer against metal from the opposite direction.

The symbols over the entrances to the side tunnels became more complex, making them more difficult to remember without a way to write them down. She stayed on the main tunnel, but there was much more to see, causing her to become more frustrated because she was afraid of getting lost.

The aroma of fresh fruit drew her attention, and she followed the scent to an open doorway. When she stepped inside, she was pleasantly surprised to see several people sitting at tables, while enjoying a pink liquid from glasses with green straws. Their conversations stopped as they turned to look at her.

"Hello. As you can see from my clothing, I'm not from around here. My name is Rhonda, and whatever you're drinking smells good. What are they?"

A middle-aged woman smiled and got up. "Hi, Rhonda. We all know who you are because of our connection. I'm Marcy. They are a variety of rehydrated fruits. You can mix them together if you like. Let me show you."

Marcy led Rhonda to a small door above a narrow stone countertop, then indicated the touch pads. "Just select which flavor you want."

"I'm sorry, but I don't understand your written language. How about strawberry?"

Marcy touched a pad, then the door opened, and she reached inside to bring out a ready to drink glass and handed it to Rhonda. "Here."

Rhonda accepted the glass and took a sip through the straw. "Umm. This is good. Where I come from, we call it a smoothie."

"What do you think of our village?"

"It's bigger than I thought it would be, and since I don't know your writing, I'm having a hard time finding my way around. What I really need is a map."

Marcy chuckled. "Let me show you something."

Rhonda held onto her drink as she followed Marcy out into the main corridor. When her new acquaintance indicated the smooth stone wall by the door, Rhonda placed her hand on the surface, and a three-dimensional map appeared on the wall. She studied the layout of the tunnels throughout the mountain, which was extensive.

"The map is on the wall near every side tunnel just so you don't get lost."

"Where is my room compared to this location?"

"What's the room number?"

"I don't know. All I remember are the three symbols above the doorway." She pointed to different symbols on the wall. "This one, this one, and this one."

Marcy pointed out a location on the map. "That's yours."

"Great. Is that white dot showing me where I am right now?"

"That's correct."

"Thanks. Would you know where I can find Janis?"

Marcy frowned as she folded her arms across her chest. "Why?"

"I just wanted to talk with him, is all. I understand he's a historian, and I'd like to learn more about your society."

"If you're thinking about joining his harem, you'd better know what you're getting into before you fall under his spell."

"I wasn't. I had no idea. I mean. Would you mind telling me what someone would be getting into?"

"I'm not allowed to tell you any details."

"You can't leave me hanging like this. I won't be able to concentrate on anything else. Please, at least tell me what you can."

Marcy looked around to make sure she could not be heard by anyone else. "This isn't the happy society you were shown on the surface."

When Marcy headed back into the room, Rhonda stared after her. She needed more information, but knew Marcy would not help. She turned to the map just as it disappeared, but when she reached out and touched the smooth wall, it appeared again.

She decided since she could not read the language, her only option was to stroll through the various tunnels to discover where everything was located. At least now she didn't need to worry about getting lost, just Marcy's warning.

***

Rhonda was headed back to her room when she saw Janis enter a side tunnel two hundred feet ahead. Since she was curious to learn the secret, she hurried to catch up with him, but stopped before entering the tunnel to study the markings above the opening. Hours ago, she had discovered by substituting letters from the English alphabet with different symbols, they made words she could remember better. As far as she could tell, it was a community bathhouse.

She hurried to her room and changed into a swimsuit under her pants and shirt, then returned to the tunnel and followed it to a door. When she opened it, warm humid air flowed across her face and hands. She stepped inside a large room with five rows of benches. Each row was divided by thin walls with six inch long pegs, and over a dozen of them supported leather clothing.

She closed the door and sat down to get undressed, then hung her clothes on the pegs and set her shoes on the seat. Now dressed in a one-piece swim suit, she moved across to the only other door, opened it, and passed through into a cloud of steam.

Closing the door caused the cloud to swirl, allowing her to see people standing a short distance away. As she moved closer, she saw the backsides of two naked women looking down at something. She stopped when she was slightly behind the two women and could see between them. Lying on a padded table was a woman on her back with her eyes closed, and Janis having intercourse with her. When the woman screamed and opened her eyes, Rhonda saw the eyeballs were completely gray.

She jumped back and fell onto her butt, then backed away on her hands and feet until the steam blocked her view. When no one seemed to notice her, she stayed on the floor in the steam. When she heard the splashing of water from further away, she slowly crawled toward the sound.

The steam was thinner above a large pool of water, allowing her to see the two women bathing the blind woman, but there was no sign of Janis. A few moments later, the three women got out of the pool, then the first two began drying off the blind woman. When she turned around, Rhonda thought the woman's gray eyes were staring into her soul.

The two women led the blind woman across the room, and Rhonda followed them. She stopped when they went through a doorway, which closed behind them, then cautiously went to the door and tried the handle. She grinned when it turned, then she opened it enough to see what was on the other side.

She was looking out over an auditorium, with an audience of nineteen naked women sitting in chairs facing the stage, where the blind woman's wrists and ankles were being strapped into a plain wooden chair. When the two women joined the audience, the blind woman began chanting while staring up at the ceiling.

The doors on the far side of the stage parted, where a strange-looking figure was silhouetted in the opening. When the person moved onto the stage, the light behind it vanished, allowing Rhonda to watch a naked man wearing an ornate full head mask approach the woman in the chair.

The blind woman continued chanting while the masked man gently grabbed her hair and held her head back, then a woman with a knife in the front row of the audience got up and approached the chair. She made a tiny slice through the curated artery on the side of the blind woman's neck, then the man let go, and the woman returned to sit with the crowd. When the masked man spoke a few words, Rhonda recognized the voice and gasped.

The woman's chanting continued for a few moments as blood ran down her chest, dripping into a trench on the ground, then the chanting stopped and her head wobbled as the bleeding slowed. When the head fell forward and the bleeding stopped, the woman with the knife got up and moved close to the woman in the chair, checking for a pulse. After the woman indicated she was dead, two other women got up and unstrapped the arms and legs, then set the body onto a simple wooden stretcher and carried it away through a side door on the stage.

When the masked man left through the back doors, the rest of the women stood up, and Rhonda realized they were leaving. She closed the door and hurried back through the steamy bath house, then entered the changing room and closed the door. It only took a moment to get dressed, and she was about to leave, when she heard the women talking and splashing in the pool.

She went back to the door and eased it open, then looked into the room. Steam blocked her view of the area where Janis had sex with a blind woman, but it was nearly gone above the pool, which looked crowded.

Ever since the woman's gray eyes seemed to stare at her, Rhonda could not stop wondering why. She knew her curiosity seemed to always get her in trouble, but she had to know what they were going to do with a murdered blind woman.

She got down onto her hands and knees and opened the door just wide enough to squeeze through, then closed it and crawled along the wall in the thick cloud of steam. As she circled the room, the conversations grew louder, sounding like they were arguing over who gets to sleep with Janis tonight. By the time she reached the door to the auditorium, she knew three women at a time would spend the night with Janis. Apparently, he was never satisfied for long, and had great stamina.

She eased the door open and crawled through, then closed it and stayed down while listening to learn if she was alone. The auditorium was quiet, so she slowly stood up and looked around. When she didn't see anyone, she hurried down to the stage and quietly opened the side door where they had taken the body.

It opened into a long tunnel, which curved down at an angle out of sight, then she went through and stopped to look behind her one last time. When she was sure she was not followed, she closed the door and hurried along the tunnel. When she reached the end, it branched off into three large tunnels going in different directions, with nothing to indicate where they go, so she entered the one going left.

One hundred feet further, she came to a wide double door, but there were no windows. She slowly pushed on one side enough to see what was going on, and a cool breeze gently moved past her face, but there was no one in the part of the room she could see.

She pushed it open enough to go through, then the door automatically closed behind her, and an electric light came on overhead. She looked around that part of the room and it was vacant, but when she turned around to the area she could not see, her jaw dropped open as she froze in shock. The skinless body of a woman with gray eyes was hanging upside down from a large hook through the skin behind her ankles.

Rhonda gagged and bent over to throw up, expelling a small amount of undigested pink liquid onto the stone floor. After the second round of gagging, she stood up and wiped the tears from her eyes and the drool from her mouth and nose on the sleeve of her shirt.

She looked away from the body and noticed a small hose coiled on the floor, so she shuffled over to find out its purpose. The only control was a squeeze nozzle on the end. She picked it up and aimed it into a trough in the stone floor, then when she pulled the handle, a clear liquid shot out, and she released her grip. She sniffed the liquid, then used her other hand to feel it with her fingertips. She sniffed it again, then touched it with the tip of her tongue and smiled when it was H_2O.

She squeezed the handle again to rinse off her hands and face, then took several swallows of water to wash out her mouth and throat. She noticed the vomit on her shoes and aimed the nozzle at them, and since they were waterproof, the vile goo was easily washed away before she shut it off and set the nozzle back down.

Now that she was over the initial shock, Rhonda studied the room for more details. The first thing she noticed was the hook holding the body was attached to a roller on an overhead track. She followed the rail system with her eyes until it disappeared above another set of double doors.

She moved closer to the red flesh of the body and noticed they had even skinned the feet and toes, the skin around the vagina, the hands and fingertips, and the skin on the neck up to the jawline. Recognizing the face made the scene surrealistic, then she noticed a dime-size hole in her right temple. She checked for a matching hole in the other side of the head, but it was still covered in skin.

She checked out the rest of the room, but it was empty, then decided to follow the overhead rails and went to the doors with small windows. Electric lights were on the other side, and once again she peered through and didn't see anyone. She entered and immediately wished she hadn't. The air reeked of sulfuric acid, but it was not unbearable. Just annoying.

She continued past a stone wall with a ten foot long, thick wooden counter. It appeared worn down in the center from years of use, but she could not imagine eating on it. She glimpsed something shiny on the other side and stopped. When she leaned over the counter, she saw a trough of running water cut into the wall. The railing was directly overhead, and she shuddered at the thought this might be where they prepared the bodies for burial.

On the other side of the narrow room were stacks of two foot square wooden boxes, with the lids stacked in columns on one side. In one corner were two-wheeled hand trucks for moving them.

She heard several pairs of footsteps approaching from the room with the body and quickly looked around for a way out. There was another set of double doors thirty feet past the counter and she hurried through one side and helped it close, then peered through the gap. Three teenage men rolled the skinless body through the first set of doors and stopped.

She waited, but they didn't move, as if in a trance. For a fraction of a second, the skin on their right temples glowed, then they lifted the body off the hook and lowered it onto the table. When one of them opened a drawer and reached inside, she expected him to bring out rubber hoses and bottles of embalming fluids. What he brought out was disgusting. The boy handed out bloody knives and saw blades.

They severed the head from the torso, then placed it in a small wooden box and set it aside. All of them began dissecting the woman, placing the parts in the wooden boxes.

The internal organs were sliced into small pieces and tossed into the trough at the back of the counter, which were washed away. Once all the body parts were in four boxes, one boy grabbed the hose and began washing off the counter, while the other two loaded the boxes in pairs stacked on two hand trucks.

Rhonda suddenly realized they would be steering the boxes out through her doors. She spun around and hurried along the tunnel until she reached the next door, which was single and appeared much stronger than the average doors. There was nowhere else to go, so she grabbed the latch and pulled.

The door opened and ice cold air rushed out, but she had no choice. She hurried inside and dragged the door closed. When she turned around, five widely spaced rows of overhead lights illuminated hundreds of two foot square wooden boxes, stacked from floor to ceiling, and appeared to go on forever.

The door suddenly opened and the two boys with the hand trucks entered. She had nowhere to hide while holding her breath, wondering what would happen next. To her surprise, they steered their loads around her as they continued down the center aisle.

They had left the door open, and she was about to run from the room when the third boy entered. She froze as he moved around her, then he suddenly stopped. When she saw the flash of light under the skin of his right temple, she hurried out of the room, then ran back along the tunnel.

She burst through the first set of double doors without looking, then continued past the wet counter and out the second set. When she reached the three branches in the tunnel, she chose the one back to the auditorium.

She didn't stop running until she reached the door from the auditorium into the community bath, then took a moment to catch her breath. During the entire run, crazy ideas about the boxes churned in her head, each more horrific than the previous one. The fact she had not seen a single domesticated animal caused her to think the worst about this utopian society. Were Janis and his followers cannibals?

She eased the door open and peered inside at the pool area. Fortunately, the women were gone, so she hurried over to the changing room. When she emerged into the main throughway, she forced her nerves to calm down and slowed her pace while she thought about what had just happened.

When she reached her room, she collapsed backward onto the bed, put her hands behind her head, then stared at the stone ceiling. "What have I gotten myself into this time?"

Chapter 22

THE ESCAPE TUNNEL:

Lieutenant Hershey and Clark were walking side by side with Patricia behind them, followed by Nancy strolling along next to Emory. Some of the overhead bulbs had burned out, creating areas of near darkness, and having to move rocks off the piles in some areas to get through was slowing them down.

Something occurred to Clark, and he glanced over his shoulder at Emory. "How come we went downhill first instead of straight?"

"I have no idea. Like I said, I've never been down here. I'll tell you this much. If you didn't notice, there is hardly any steel rebar in the concrete. It's no wonder the tunnels collapsed so easily."

Clark suddenly stopped next to a six foot tall by eight foot wide steel frame in the concrete wall. It was eight inches deep, where a single sheet of rusted metal blocked the way through. When he tapped it with his knuckles, it was solid, then Emory moved up beside him. "Any idea where this goes?"

Emory saw there were no hinges or a handle. "I have no idea, but we're not getting in."

Clark looked at his wristwatch and pressed a tiny button on the side, then numbers appeared. "We've gone five miles so far."

Nancy heard him and looked over at Emory. "Do you remember how long this tunnel is?"

"Not exactly. I know it wasn't straight. Some engineers I talked to said there were several places where they had to make some detours to avoid hazardous areas, but it was at least thirty miles."

Patricia suddenly turned and bumped into Emory, then glared at him. "Watch where you're going!"

"But you're the one."

"Just shut up, janitor! You said it was twenty miles to the exit. Were you lying to me?"

"No, Ma'am. I said it was twenty miles to the exit by road. And I'm a custodian, not a janitor."

"Well, you should have been more specific."

Hershey and Clark were ten feet ahead of the VP when they stopped to listen. When she turned around and began walking again, they received a scathing look from her as she continued past them.

Nancy stopped beside her brother to look at Hershey. "What's up with her?"

"She's scared. The way I understand it, she didn't want to be here, but was ordered to do so by the president."

Patricia stopped walking and spun around. "I can hear you. Yes, I was forced to come here, and yes, I'm a little frightened. Now that you know, can we continue?"

When the group began moving, Emory held back until the others were between him and the VP. He decided if all she was going to do was cut him down, he would stay away from her.

Patricia was moving through an area with three burned out light bulbs in a row, and was staring at the small mound of rubble beneath the next glowing light. Her next step was into empty space and she lost her balance, screaming as she fell forward into darkness. A hand grabbed her wrist and her arm felt like it was being ripped from the socket when she suddenly stopped falling.

Clark gritted his teeth, desperately squeezing the VP's wrist with one hand while he lay partway over the edge of the tunnel. Two hands suddenly reached around his arm and the weight was gone, then he rolled onto his side out of the way while Hershey hauled the VP back onto the floor.

Nancy knelt down and helped her brother sit up, then removed his backpack for him. She looked over at the VP, who was on her hands and knees while calming her nerves, with Emory and Hershey standing over her. Nancy got up and looked down at Clark, who had grabbed his penlight and crawled to the edge to look down. "What do you see?"

"The floor collapsed and is about fifteen feet down. It's covered in large rocks, so we can't jump to the bottom."

Nancy aimed her own beam of light at the other side, revealing a twenty foot wide space to get across if they wanted to continue. She aimed it at the left side wall, which was hanging precariously over the twenty foot wide gap between them and the other side of the tunnel, with no way to get across. She aimed it at the right side wall, which also hung over the gap, but it had an eight inch wide ledge to stand on. "I'm the smallest, so I'll go first and you can toss my backpack across to me."

Hershey quickly slid her pack to the floor, then held her hand out to Nancy. "It should be me. I'm the biggest. If it can support my weight, it will be okay for all of you to cross. Let me use your light to check out where I need to step."

Hershey accepted the penlight and moved close to the edge of the right wall. First, she looked over the side at the ledge, two feet below. "The first step will be tricky, and there are a few gaps."

She moved back and studied the wall above the ledge, searching for handholds. A few small shadowed areas appeared on the surface, but when Clark's light hit them at a different angle, they seemed to disappear.

Clark aimed his light in a different direction and the shadows from Hershey's light appeared again, then he moved around to her side. "I guess we'll need to feel our way across, but at least there are some places the hold on to."

Hershey turned off her light and slid it into her shirt pocket, then knelt down and held onto the floor as she stepped down onto the ledge. She reached up and ran her fingers across the surface of the cement wall to a shadow and felt a shallow recessed area, then used her fingertips for balance while side-stepping across the narrow concrete ledge.

Clark aimed the beam of his light slightly ahead of the Lieutenant so she could see where to step, exposing two and a half feet of missing ledge. She easily leapt across, then stepped up onto the floor on the other side.

Hershey turned around and smiled at the group. "Nothing to it. Start tossing the packs and I'll catch them."

Clark easily hurled Hershey's smaller soft pack across the gap. Hershey caught it and set it aside, then held her hands out for the next one. He grabbed the aluminum frame of his pack and threw it next, with the Lieutenant catching it like an NFL linebacker, then he did the same with Nancy's pack.

When Clark reached out for the last backpack, Emory appeared apprehensive about handing it over, but gave it up. It was a soft pack like Hershey's but felt heavier, and he added a little more force when he heaved it across. When it nearly soared over Hershey's head, he heard Emory gasp, and turned to face him. "What's in your backpack?"

"A glass bottle of expensive blended whiskey."

"Are you serious?"

"You never know when it might come in handy." He turned to the VP. "I bet you could have used a shot a few minutes ago."

"I'm fine, and I'm next."

Hershey watched Clark hold on to the VP's hand as she stepped down onto the ledge. "Remember, the last missing section of the ledge is shorter than it will look from your perspective, and I'll be here to help you across."

Patricia took a few deep breaths, then reached up for a shadowed area with her right hand. When her fingertips had a firm grip, she side-stepped across the ledge and stopped to switch hands and reach out for another handhold. She was doing fine until she reached the missing section and stopped. "I can't jump sideways that far using only one leg."

Hershey was standing beside the wall and knelt down as she held her hand out to her boss. "It's closer than it looks, and I'll grab you."

"Okay."

Patricia concentrated on how far to jump, then just as she leapt across, realized she had forgotten to look for a place to grab the wall again. Her foot landed, then she clawed at the concrete for a handhold and sensed she was falling backward. A hand suddenly grabbed her arm to pull her back onto the ledge, then across the last two feet up onto the floor.

Hershey let go, and the VP dropped to her hands and knees again. "You don't seem to be having any luck today, Ma'am."

Patricia rolled onto her butt and looked up at the Lieutenant. "So it seems."

Emory was looking across at the women when the VP suddenly gave him an imploring stare. "Help yourself."

Emory watched her drag his pack over and open the flap, then grinned when she brought out the pint of golden liquid. When she opened the cap and took a small swallow, he smiled.

Patricia put the cap back on the bottle and placed it into the pack, then felt a warm sensation course through her body. She remained on her butt while watching the others come across without problems, then got up. She felt the tension in her shoulders disappearing, then reached down to pick up Emory's pack for him. "That was my first drink of alcohol in five years." When he accepted his pack, she turned to the others and began walking. "Onward."

Emory stared after her as she continued along the tunnel, wondering why she had not even smiled or shown some sign of gratitude. He turned away from the others as he swung the pack onto his shoulders. "You're welcome."

When Emory stomped past her, Nancy knew how he was feeling, and could not understand why the VP was not showing him any respect or gratitude. While Hershey and Clark were putting on their backpacks, she grabbed hers and slid it over her shoulders as she hurried to catch up with Emory.

Emory was frowning while watching the back of the VP as they crawled over another pile of rubble shaken loose from the ceiling. "What's your problem with me?"

Patricia reached the top of the pile, but didn't look back. "I don't know what you're talking about."

Emory's jaw clinched shut to control his frustration as he followed her down the other side. He realized she was moving even faster than before, so he ran past her and turned around to make her stop. "That's enough!"

Nancy was coming down the other side of the pile when she saw what was happening. Her new friend appeared to be arguing with the Vice President of the United States of America, so she hurried over to join them.

Patricia stopped and stared up at Emory standing in front of her, ready to order him out of the way, when Nancy suddenly moved past her to join him. A moment later, Hershey and Clark were standing with them, all staring at her.

Nancy moved between Emory and the VP. "We've all noticed your attitude toward him. Could you at least tell us why?"

Patricia crossed her arms over her chest and looked away. "For generations my family members worked hard doing jobs no one else wanted to do, with little respect in return." She turned back to look at them. "My mother broke the mold to become an attorney, which afforded me the opportunity to become the Vice President. Being with you reminds me of everything I didn't want anyone to know about my family history."

Emory shoved Nancy out of the way to look into the eyes of the VP. "Listen, little lady. I'm as proud of what I've accomplished here at this facility as you are about your job. When I look at you, I see a pampered little girl who's mad at the world for her insecurities."

"You don't know me well enough to make that kind of judgment."

"I've seen enough of your social media postings to get a pretty good idea of your likes and dislikes."

"I fight for what I believe in."

"I thought you were supposed to fight for what the American people wanted?"

"The majority of them must believe the same as me or I would not have been elected as VP."

"Listen, little princess. You were not elected. You were selected by the big man because he needed your followers to vote for him. You're a politician, so you know how it works."

Patricia stared back at him for a moment, then looked away and began walking again. She could feel the effects of the alcohol causing her anxiety to decrease a little, otherwise she would have continued to argue with Emory over the merits of her beliefs.

Emory stared at the floor for a moment, then turned and continued behind the VP without speaking. He sensed someone beside him, then looked over at Nancy, who grinned at him for a moment before looking ahead. He glanced back over his shoulder, where the Lieutenant and Clark were strolling side by side behind them, then turned back and sighed with relief he wasn't alone with the VP.

Chapter 23

WINDANCER:

Geneva looked through the open doorway of Marcus's cabin and saw him sitting up in bed while reading a book. It seemed like only yesterday she had hated him for dragging her away from her friends. Now she was relieved he was getting better and realized how much she cared about him now.

When she knocked on the door frame, he looked up at her and smiled, and she smiled in return. "Hey, Grandpa. What are you reading?"

"It's something I wrote over ten years ago."

"Is that when you were a volcanologist?"

Marcus closed the book, then waved Geneva over to a chair next to his bed. She entered the room and turned the chair around to face him, he waited until she sat down. "Yeah, and it seems a lifetime ago."

She smirked at him. "Thirty years *is* a lifetime."

He chuckled. "I suppose so."

"What is it about?"

"It's an article I wrote being quoted in this book. It's the possible ramifications of what could happen. Or rather, what will happen if we don't stop more volcanoes from erupting."

"What are we supposed to do about it? The computer wizzes underground can't stop it."

Brian had overheard the conversation from the salon and had moved to the doorway. "I would be interested in any knowledge you may have that could stop this."

Marcus set the book down on the nightstand and studied his guest. "All right. We are on the Tronador Volcano, and the underground tunnels where your society is living are the result of those past eruptions. It's inactive at the moment, but I believe if it becomes active again, it might be enough to relieve the pressure on the other volcanoes and end the eruptions and earthquakes."

Brian could not believe what he was hearing. "You can't be serious! An entire civilization, not to mention the incredible knowledge we have, will be destroyed. If my people and their technology survive, we can start over. Maybe even make it a better society than you had."

"That's a big maybe."

"So is your idea of causing it to erupt."

***

Olivia was in Rickie's room, sitting beside her daughter's bed while holding her hand. With Brian's help, she had gotten the bullet out of Rickie's butt cheek. There was no serious damage, but it would be sore for a while. The bullet had gone cleanly through Oscar's shoulder, and after bandaging his wounds, he took over standing guard in the pilothouse.

When Olivia heard Brian's raised voice coming from her father's cabin, she felt Rickie's hand tighten on hers and knew what she wanted. "I'll go find out."

Rickie let go. "Leave the door open."

Olivia got up and hurried past her cabin to her father's, easing Brian out of the way so she could step inside the room. "What's going on?"

Brian folded his arms across his chest. "Your father wants to commit genocide against an intelligent and innocent society."

Geneva got out of the chair and stood toe to toe with the visitor. "Don't tell me that crap! I saw your ceremony with the masked man in the woods last night." She turned to Marcus. "During some kind of ritual, they had a blind man strapped to a chair while he was pleading for help. Another man in a fancy headdress and mask had one of his slaves cut the blind man's throat. Oh, and guess what? The masked man was Janis."

Brian kept his arms crossed. "If he wore a mask, how do you know it was Janis?"

"He talked in a strange language during the ritual, and when we met him underground before we left, I recognized his voice."

"I don't believe you."

"Yeah, that's what I thought you'd say."

Olivia got Geneva's attention. "Why didn't you say something about it to Rhonda?"

"I tried, but it was hard to convince her not to go without sounding crazy. You believe me, don't you?"

"Of course, but you're right about Rhonda. She was smitten by his charm, as was I."

Geneva turned to look down the hallway when she heard Rickie yell, 'me too', then turned back to Marcus. "They are murderers and not worth saving, and I say we start an eruption. What do I need to do?"

Olivia signaled for Marcus not to speak. "Hold on a second, Dad. You want to cause an eruption? I thought you said if another major volcano erupts, everyone dies."

"You're correct, I did say that, but here's the difference. There are two types of eruptions in terms of activity. Explosive and effusive. Explosive eruptions, like Mount Saint Helens and Yellowstone, are characterized by gas-driven explosions that propel magma and tephra. Effusive eruptions, on the other hand, are characterized by the outpouring of lava without significant explosive eruptions, like in Hawaii. This one is effusive, and all the magma will flow to the ocean."

Brian lowered his arms to his sides. "Yes, and it will destroy an entire civilization."

Marcus realized he had no choice but to try. "I know, and I'm sorry."

After hearing Geneva's story about the ritual, Olivia decided to ask a question that had been bothering her since they met Nina. "I understand you don't have domesticated livestock, so I was wondering where you find animals large enough to make pants from a single piece of leather?"

"We don't know where our clothes come from."

"Haven't you ever wondered how come they seem tailored to fit your body?"

"They are recycled. It's just the way things have worked for thousands of years, and no one questions why."

Geneva was staring out through the rear window and noticed the ash had started falling again, then she sat back down next to Marcus. "We're running out of time, Grandpa. Tell me what I need to do to cause an eruption."

"You can't do it on your own, and none of us are capable of helping you."

Brian held his hand up. "I'll help, Geneva."

She stared at him. "You're one of them, and I can't trust you."

"I've heard rumors about Janis and his followers. He believes in the ancient ways and craves power, but I'm not like them. I'm with Daniela, and believe we are more intelligent than our ancient ancestors."

"Oh, yeah? Well, I heard everyone is hooked up to your computer, and you can't trust your thoughts are your own. You might give away our plan and your people will try to stop me."

"It's true, we are all connected to the computer through our neural implants, but it doesn't control anyone. Although some of us *have* noticed a significant increase in the number of people becoming Janis followers, but no one knows how he is convincing them to join him."

Geneva threw her hands into the air in frustration. "For people who instantly have the answers to every question imaginable available in your heads, you're not very smart. Janis must be manipulating the computer to force people to join him."

"No one can control the computer, but I've noticed more glows than normal."

The word glow got Geneva's attention. "What's a glow?"

Brian took a moment to think about how best to describe it. "Our connection to the computer is through an implant in our right temple. Normally it's inactive, but when we initiate a connection, it radiates light through the thin skin."

"How far away do you have to go before you lose the connection?"

"Warriors have reported losing the link once they left the hidden lava tunnel we took to get here."

"I saw that happen to all the people in the audience during the ritual, but it was like Janis was controlling them."

"What do you mean? You said you did not see his face."

"Okay, his mask turned and faced the audience, then all their glow balls came on at the same time. Listen. That doesn't matter anymore. Tell me how to cause this mountain to barf."

Marcus was proud of the way Geneva was behaving, but hated the idea of sending her back on her own. "Okay. If you can get to the computer, you need to find a way to shut down the steam to the heat exchangers. Once the pressure is released, they'll explode, allowing the magma to flow to the surface."

Geneva turned to Brian. "How can I get there undetected?"

"It is not possible. By the time you get back, the main door to the underground tunnels will be locked. You cannot even get started."

"Let's say I get in. What next?"

"Almost everyone will be in the lower levels, and that won't be a problem in the main thruway. About three hundred yards in, one of the doors on the right is an elevator to the lower levels."

"Hey, I know where that is. We were there before we left."

Olivia remembered something else from their visit. "Our guide used her palm to open the doors. Will our palms work?"

Brian looked at his right hand and rotated the slender ring on his little finger, then looked at everyone staring at him. "Now you want to make me part of this Armageddon?"

Olivia placed her hand on Brian's shoulder. "I know you don't like the idea of killing all those below ground, but it's for the sake of the entire planet."

Brian shoved his hands under the top of his pants. "No. I won't do it. You'll just have to figure a way to do it without my help."

Geneva brought the knife out from her back pocket, flipping the blade out while shoving it in front of Brian's face. "I already figured out how to do it without your help. That ring must be a controller. I'll just cut off your finger and take it."

Brian's jaw dropped as he looked around at the others for a sign they would stop Geneva. When they just stared back, he closed his mouth and pulled his hands out of his pants. He slid a thin ring off his little finger, then held it out to Geneva. "Fine. Here. Take it."

Geneva put her knife away with one hand while taking the ring in the other. "Anything special I need to do to make it work?"

"No. Just hold it against the panel."

Olivia knew he was holding something back. "What about the code to make the elevator work?"

"I do not know it."

Geneva slid the ring into her front pocket. "It's seven, zero, five, five, two, one, six. Okay. I'll lower the skiff and get started."

Marcus reached out and grabbed her hand. "You should take a gun with you."

"I don't want to kill anyone. I have my knife, so I'll be okay."

Brian moved closer to Geneva. "Perhaps you are correct, but how will you get through the locked door?"

She grinned at her grandpa. "I keep lock picking sets under the laces of my shoes for emergencies. You never know when you need to break into someplace for supplies."

Chapter 24

THE CAVE:

Rhonda was in her room, lying on her cot while staring up at the ceiling, when the door suddenly opened and Janis walked in, so she got up and stared at him. "I saw your ceremony. I also saw what they did to her body, and I want to know what's going on."

Janis sat on one end of the cot and indicated for her to sit down beside him, but she folded her arms over her chest. "I didn't force you to stay here."

"Yes, but you didn't tell me you sacrifice people."

"This is the way it has been for thousands of generations. We recycle everything, including human bodies."

Rhonda thought she already knew the answer, but had to ask. "What about your clothes? Are they made from recycled materials?"

"Once we outgrow them, they are put into circulation for someone else to wear."

"What I mean is, are they made from human skin?"

"Of course. But like all things, they eventually wear out and need to be replaced. The living body is just a shell for supporting consciousness. There is no sense in wasting it."

"What about all the body parts you have in the freezer?"

Janis smirked at her. "Some of us have the privilege of eating meat. Did you see any domesticated animals down here?"

"That's sickening! What about the ceremony? You killed that woman."

"Did you see her eyes?"

"Yes, they were gray."

"She was blind and willingly gave her body up to be recycled."

"She looked too young to go blind."

"Yes, she was only forty-nine. It's one of the possible side effects of the neural implants being so close to the eyes, but it's the only way to connect to the computer."

"Is everyone connected?"

"Of course. After our first major meeting an hour from now, someone will come to take you to get your implant installed."

"I don't want an implant."

"Now that you're staying with us, you have no choice. Don't worry. Once it's activated, you'll understand and agree it's the best way for all of us to get along."

"I don't want any part of this, and I'm leaving."

Janis leapt off the cot and blocked her way to the door. "You're not going anywhere. Sit down!"

Rhonda thought about fighting him to get out, but realized his followers would stop her before she made it back to the surface. She sat down and looked up at him. "How do you know the implant will work on me?"

"I don't, but that won't stop us from trying."

Rhonda turned away from him to stare at the wall. She heard the door close, then what sounded like metal scraping metal. When she turned back, Janis was gone. She leapt up and tried the doorknob, but it didn't turn.

She plopped back down on the cot with her back against the wall, frustrated she had decided to stay. It sounded like multiple footfalls outside in the walkway, and several conversations getting louder, then quieter. After a few minutes, there was no sound.

She was looking at her shoes when she suddenly remembered what Geneva had given her. She grinned and moved her left foot within reach, then untied the laces and slid the two skinny pieces of flat metal from beneath the flap, and put them between her lips while retying her shoe.

She got up and went to the door, then knelt down and inserted the lock picking tools below the doorknob. She moved them around until she heard the click, then took them out and grabbed the knob. When it turned, she smiled and slid the tools into her back pocket, then eased the door open. There was no one in sight, so she when through and closed it behind her before heading back to the main tunnel.

When she came around a curved wall leading to the exit into the cavern, she heard a familiar female voice and a strange man's voice coming from the area near the main door. She slowly moved around the curve until she saw the back of a warrior aiming a spear at Geneva, who was holding a knife out toward the man. Behind Geneva, the massive main door was open.

She remembered passing a shop displaying ceramic utensils and dishware a short distance away, then ran back and went inside the deserted room. She grabbed a large ceramic pot and ran back to the exit, then slowly approached the back of the warrior.

She raised the pot to clobber the warrior on the back of the head when Geneva made the mistake of looking past him at her. When he spun around, she slammed the pot against his forehead. He staggered back but didn't go down until Geneva kicked the back of his knees to drive his legs out from under him.

Geneva watched the back of the warrior's head slam onto the stone floor, then he stopped moving. She turned to Rhonda, who rushed forward and wrapped her arms around her neck, hugging her tightly.

Rhonda let go and stepped back, then wiped the tears from her cheeks with the back of her hand. "You were right. I never should have stayed. So, why are you here?"

"I'm going to blow up the heat exchangers and cause this volcano to erupt."

Rhonda stared at her for a moment while comprehending the magnitude of what she wanted to do. "I thought we wanted to stop the eruptions?"

"Marcus said we can relieve the pressure on the other volcanoes by making this one release a bunch of magma."

Rhonda looked at the open exit door, then back along the main tunnel. "If we're going to do this, we need to go now while everyone is in the auditorium."

As they hurried along the main tunnel, Rhonda looked over at Geneva. "How do you plan on getting into the elevator?"

"We have two new passengers, and I took a ring from a finger that will let me open the door."

"What did you do with the finger?"

"I let him keep it."

Rhonda smirked at her friend, then she heard someone coming up the tunnel, and pulled Geneva into a side door. They waited as another warrior strolled past, then quietly moved back into the tunnel and continued.

When they reached the elevator door, Geneva brought out the ring and placed it against the smooth surface of the stone wall. The door opened, they hurried inside, then Geneva rushed over and pushed a series of buttons on the control pad. The door closed, and the humidity began to drop.

When the elevator began descending, Rhonda grinned at her friend. "Did the passengers tell you what to do when we reach the computer?"

"No, but Marcus said I need to set the timer on the primary pressure relief valve to open after we leave this place. Hopefully, it's enough time to get back to the *Windancer*."

"Where is it?"

"Near the beach where we spent the night."

"That's a long way. I take it you used the skiff to get here?"

"Yeah, but the ash is falling pretty good now, which is making it harder to see what's ahead."

The elevator stopped, then the door opened, and they stepped out into the master control room they had visited earlier. Geneva moved up to the control console but did not recognize any of the markings, then turned to Rhonda. "I don't understand any of these symbols."

Rhonda moved up beside her and studied the controls. "What did he say, exactly?"

"He said Sheryl showed him the symbol for the pressure regulator controls and it looked like an arrowhead."

Rhonda checked all the symbols, but didn't see it. "Are you sure?"

"Yeah, that's what he said."

Rhonda noticed a smaller console against the wall and went over to check it out, then smiled and turned to Geneva. "Here it is."

Geneva moved over beside her and looked at the controls. When she placed the ring on the console, a cover opened, then a touch screen picture appeared with a series of green numbers flashing at the top. "Do you understand any of this?"

"Some of it."

Rhonda tapped a few places on the image and the numbers at the top stopped flashing. She tapped several symbols, then the green symbols turned red, and appeared to be counting down, so she stepped back and looked at Geneva. "If my understanding is correct, we have two hours before the heat exchangers blow."

"Then we should make a run for it."

They entered the elevator and Geneva used the ring on the controls, then touched the buttons to take them to the top. When the door opened, the humid air rushed in as they stepped out and looked around. When they didn't see anyone, they began running up the tunnel.

When they reached the exit door, the warrior was still unconscious, but when Rhonda started to go through the doorway, Geneva suddenly had an idea and stopped her. "Let's drag him to the other side and I'll lock it. That way, they might not know we were here."

They each grabbed one of the warrior's arms and hauled him through the opening, then Geneva closed the door and knelt in front of it to set the lock. A moment later, she got up and indicated it was time to leave.

They ran into the cavern and headed for the entrance when a thought occurred to Rhonda. "Did anyone try to stop you on your way here?"

"No. The place is deserted."

They jogged through the opening into lightly falling gray flakes of ash until they entered the darkness of the tunnel. They slowed down while their eyes adjusted to the dim light from the algae, giving them time for their muscles to recuperate from the run.

Something suddenly occurred to Geneva. "Why didn't we set off any alarms when you tweaked the system?"

"I'm not sure. Maybe the alarms don't go off until the pressure relief valve blows." She looked at her wristwatch. "That will be in one hour and thirty-two minutes, give or take."

"You don't seem to upset about it. Did something happen between you and Janis?"

"You would not believe me if I told you how bad things got."

"Did you see the ceremony?"

Rhonda grabbed Geneva's arm as she stopped. "How do you know about it?"

Geneva eased her arm out of Rhonda's grasp. "That first night, I saw a ceremony where he killed a man. That's what I was trying to tell you."

"I wish you would have tried harder."

Geneva began walking. "I saw the way you were looking at him. You wouldn't have believed me."

Rhonda heaved a deep sigh of frustration as she caught up with her friend. "You're probably right. He was a charmer. Are you ready to run again?"

"Hell yeah. Let's get out of here."

Chapter 25

THE FACILITY REC ROOM:

Jackson and Sargent Kellerman had left the soldiers playing cards to check the damage in the main tunnel, and were moving a few large rocks off the top of the pile in front of the mess hall. When all the movable stones and chunks of concrete were off the pile, they took a break.

Jackson was checking out a massive block of concrete, which was leaning against the double doors into the mess hall, when he realized something was missing. "I'm not an engineer, but shouldn't there be a lot more metal rods in this concrete?"

"I noticed that, too. I wonder if it's that way in the entire facility."

He noticed the trace of blood seeping through the bandage around Kellerman's hand. "You need to be more careful."

"I'll be fine, Doctor."

"Call me Jackson. It appears we're not going to be getting a decent meal today."

The Sargent grinned. "After some of the food I've tasted over the past three days, this might be a good thing."

"I'm sure there was something in there worth eating."

"It wasn't the food, it was the cook. I mean, who puts canned peas and creamed corn in with canned beef and call it a casserole."

Jackson turned away from the pile and headed back toward the rec room. "I'll admit, it doesn't sound very appetizing."

"I agree. I would have used canned chicken or even tuna."

The ground moved so fast they both lost their balance, grabbing each other as they crashed onto the hard ground. Their bodies rolled with the shaking as more cracks formed across the concrete ceiling, then the crashing of chunks of gray rocks hitting the floor was heard over the rumble of the quake.

The shaking slowed and stopped, as did the rumble, but the occasional shattering of concrete continued for a few moments. When it stopped, Jackson slowly sat up to look around. As the dust settled onto the floor, he realized the main lighting was off, and the soft glowing orbs were the emergency lights.

***

ESCAPE TUNNEL:

With the ground shaking, Emory had trouble keeping his face over the back of the VP's head and his body over hers, while chunks of concrete, rocks, and dirt bounce off his arms and the back of his legs. The shaking stopped, and the debris stopped falling, but he kept his eyelids squeezed shut to block the dust as he rolled off her body, with his pack padding his back from the sharp rocks.

The weight on her back was suddenly gone, and Patricia opened her eyes, then slowly rolled over, grimacing when rocks poked into her backside. She sat up sideways in the total darkness, then used her hand to brush away the debris from under her butt before sitting flat on the ground. "Can anyone hear me?"

Emory opened his eyes to stare at the ceiling, and for a moment, thought he was blind. "I hear you. Hold on a second while I get my flashlight."

Emory slid his butt sideways to clear an area beneath him, then sat up without more pain. He slipped the pack off his shoulders and reached inside, then brought out a penlight and flipped it on. First, he aimed it at the VP, then at the ground, the walls, and up at the fractured ceiling.

He suddenly remembered the others and swung the light back along the tunnel, over a thirty-foot gap to the other side. "Can anyone hear me?"

When no one answered, he swept away the rubble to place his hands on the ground, then stood up and aimed the beam at the floor. He reached down and took the VP's hand to help her up, then flashed the light over her body to make sure she was okay. "Anything broken?"

Under the light, she studied the few bleeding cuts on her arms and hands, then noticed the blood running down the side of Emory's head. "No, I don't think so. Let me have the flashlight."

Emory did as asked, then she grabbed his shoulder and pulled him over to check his head. He grimaced but remained still as she used her fingers to part his hair. "Do you see something wrong?"

Patricia used one hand to move his hair out of the way while studying his head in the light. "Yes, three cuts in your scalp. It looks like they stopped bleeding for now. Do they hurt?"

"Only when you pull on them."

Patricia stopped searching for more cuts and lowered her hands. As Emory straightened up, she carefully moved to the edge of the concrete floor, then aimed the light over the side and gasped. "Where did they go?"

Emory moved up beside her and looked over the edge at the mound of dirt and rock fifty feet below. He reached over and gently grasped the VP's hand holding the light, then moved it to shine the beam at the ceiling, which was twenty feet higher than the tunnel, then he let go. "They must be buried underneath that pile."

Patricia aimed the light down and leaned over the edge to holler. "Is anyone still alive?"

When no one answered, she leaned back and aimed the light into Emory's eyes before he held his hand up to block it, so she aimed it at his chest. "Sorry."

"There's nothing we can do for them, and we can't go back. I guess we keep going."

Patricia slowly turned around, then kept the light aimed at the rock covered floor as she moved to Emory's backpack. She reached down to grab it, then held it out to him. "I don't know about you, but I could use a shot of whiskey right now."

Emory set the pack down while the VP aimed the light at it, then he reached inside and brought out the small bottle. He opened the cap, then held it out to her. When she grabbed it, he waited while she took a much larger drink than the last time before handing it back. He took a small swallow, then replaced the cap and put it away. "We should be getting close to the exit."

"I just hope the rest of the tunnel hasn't collapsed."

Emory slid the backpack over his shoulders, then the VP led the way through the debris. "Onward."

***

REC ROOM:

Jackson looked around for Kellerman, whose face was against the only smooth spot on the ground. He was about to reach out to see if she was okay when she placed her hands against the concrete and pushed herself up.

Kellerman shook the small rocks and dust out of her hair, then looked at Jackson. "That was a big one."

Jackson suddenly stood up, then reached down to help Kellerman. "The soldiers!"

They hurried over chunks of concrete and loose gravel to the double doors, then each shoved one side open as they rushed into the room. Gray dust filled the air as they made their way over to the table with the card game, as Private Sterns helped Tremble and Renner out from underneath it.

Gustavo was kneeling over the unconscious woman on the couch, and Jackson went over to see if they were all right. "Are either of you hurt?"

"Not seriously. My back was hit by a couple of rocks while I was covering her, but I'm okay, and so is she. Except for the part about her still being out of it."

Jackson knelt next to Tremble, who was grimacing in pain, to check the bandage on his leg for new bleeding, and it appeared the stitches of sewing thread were holding. "I wish we had something to give you for the pain."

"It'll pass, Doctor. I'll be okay."

Jackson stood as Renner got up and indicated he was fine, then he studied the room for damage, which appeared to be far less than he had expected. The soldiers had already cleared away the ceiling tiles from the last quake. Now only small pieces of concrete littered the overturned furniture and floor.

Sargent Kellerman was setting the chairs upright when she noticed Jackson's inspection. "They must have used more rebar when they built this part of the facility."

When she heard boulders tumbling in the main tunnel, Kellerman moved to the doors and pushed one side open, then stepped outside the room. A fresh cloud of dust dulled the emergency lights, making it nearly dark in the tunnel.

She heard another large chunk of stone roll down the pile leading to the exit, just as a bright light appeared to escape from a hole, bouncing around the interior of the tunnel. She smiled as she quickly made her way through the rubble to the side of the pile of dirt, rock, and concrete. "We're in here!"

The beam of light shrank to a small opening through the rocks near the ceiling, then more stones and rubble slid down the pile. The gap between the ceiling and the rocks increased, then a flashlight preceded a person through, who slid down the pile to her. "Private Burley?"

"Yeah, Sarge, it's me. We didn't know if there was anyone still alive on the other side of this pile of junk, but that last earthquake loosened it up, and most of it on the other side slid to the bottom."

"It's great to see you. Is there a way to the surface?"

"Yeah, we got through an hour ago. Who's with you?"

"Doctor Atwater, Tremble, Renner, Sterns, Gustavo, and Gardner, who has been unconscious the entire time. What about the rest of you?"

"Nothing serious. We didn't get that much damage, but we lost contact with operations."

"Okay. I'll get some help and start moving the rocks from this side while your people do the same."

"You got it, Sarge. Glad you're all alive. Hey, wait. What about the VP and the Lieutenant?"

"There was an old abandoned part of the facility no one knew about, except old man Emory. He said it could be a way out, so the Lieutenant took him, the VP, and the Atwater kids to try to get some help. I take it you haven't seen them yet."

"Nope. Okay, I'll go back through and we'll get started."

"Thanks, Burley."

***

ESCAPE TUNNEL:

When the beam of light reflected off a dull metal surface directly ahead, Patricia suddenly stopped walking, as did Emory beside her. "This must be the way out."

She tried to see out through a five-inch square glass in the door, then wiped the film off it with her hand and tried again. "It's definitely the exit. This glass is at least two inches thick, and we'll never break it."

"Let me have the light."

Emory took it from her fingers, then knelt in front of the two deadbolt locks in the door. One was locked from the outside, and he grabbed the oval-shaped knob and tried to turn it, but it didn't move. He handed the light to the VP, then used the fingers of both hands on the knob to turn it, but nothing happened.

He remained on his knees as he brought the key out from his front pants pocket. "Give me some light on the other lock, please."

He inserted the tip of the key into the lock, but the rest would not slide into the tumbler. He tried sliding it in and out a few times without luck, then he got up and looked at the VP. "I should have brought some oil instead of booze."

Patricia had an idea, grabbed the door handle, then groaned under the strain as she yanked on it several times. She stopped when the only thing that moved were the fine flakes of rust from around the doorjamb. "All this way and we can't get out!"

Emory slid the backpack from his shoulders and set it on the ground, then removed the small blanket protecting his pint of whiskey. He held onto the bottle while setting the blanket on the ground a few feet away, then sat on his pack and leaned back against the door as he twisted the cap off.

Patricia was studying the rusted seam around the doorjamb when she caught the aroma of alcohol. She turned around and didn't see Emory, then aimed the light lower and saw him sitting against the door, holding the bottle out to her.

Emory indicated the blanket. "You might as well take a load off and have a drink."

Patricia slowly squatted down onto the blanket and accepted the bottle, then leaned back against the wall and took a long swallow. "You know, if all alcohol tasted this good and was this smooth, I probably would not have been able to quit. Now it seems it won't matter, so I might as well get drunk."

Emory slowly reached over and gently took the bottle from her hand. "Fine, just don't get plastered too fast or we won't remember what we talk about."

"What's there to talk about? We have nothing in common, and our topics won't be interesting to the other person."

"You'd be surprised how much we all have in common. What's your favorite color?"

"Are you serious? You want to play questions and answers with me right now? Okay. I'm thinking of an animal."

Emory took a swallow and smiled at the flavor. "This is my own special blend. I've had friends tell me to bottle it and sell it, but I won't do it. It's just for my own enjoyment with my friends and family."

"I wondered why it didn't have a label. I'd buy it if I was still a drinker, that is."

Emory enjoyed the silence for a few minutes, hearing the occasional stone hitting the ground. "I hope the lieutenant and the kids didn't suffer."

"Yes, me too."

***

THE FACILITY:

Jackson stepped through the concrete opening into the dulled sunlight and sighed with relief he was free. He looked around and there was no color. Every surface was covered in a thin layer of gray for as far as he could see, but at the moment, the ash was not falling.

He looked over at the row of vehicles, where the Sargent and her people were cleaning up one of the trucks. As promised, she and some of her soldiers were going to take him to the exit from the abandoned tunnel. There was still no contact with the commanders because of the downed power and communication lines, but the static electricity in the ash cloud was diminishing, and they should be able to make contact by radio before he returns.

He heard the engine start and headed toward the truck, where two soldiers he didn't recognize climbed into the rear seat. He climbed up into the front passenger seat next to Kellerman, who was driving. "I couldn't tell where the road is under the ash."

"Don't worry. I know the way."

Moments later, Jackson could tell they were not driving on a maintained road, if they were even still on one. The truck bounced through ruts and pot holes impossible to see beneath the layer of ash as they covered miles of eroded mountains.

***

ESCAPE TUNNEL:

Emory felt the VP's hand sliding across his as she took the bottle from him, then he looked over at her while she stared at the golden liquid inside. It was the third time she held it for a few moments before taking a drink.

Patricia stopped looking into the bottle and turned to face Emory. "We're going to die in here, aren't we?"

He noticed the slur in her words. "I suppose so."

Patricia took a long swallow, then handed the bottle back to Emory. "Well, this trip totally sucked."

Emory was about to take a drink when he heard a quiet thud above his head. The next thud was louder, then the third thud sent tiny squares of glass raining down on their heads. He instinctively rolled to the side of the door, grabbing the VP's hand to pull her away from the shattering window, then they watched as a large hook was shoved through and slid over the edge of the door.

The screech of tortured metal hurt their ears as the door suddenly vanished, leaving a wide beam of sunlight shining through the opening. The silhouette of a person appeared, who stepped through and held a hand down to them.

"Welcome to the real world, Madam Vice President."

Patricia recognized Jackson and reached up to grab his hand, then stood up to wrap her arms around his neck. "Thank you! You just saved my life!"

Emory reached up to take the Sargent's hand and stood. "I didn't think I'd see you again, Sargent. Thanks for getting me out of here."

Jackson smelled the alcohol in the VP's breath as he eased her back and looked into her eyes. "Where are my children?"

Patricia felt woozy as she stared back at him. "I'm sorry, Jackson."

Jackson looked over at the sad look in Emory's eyes. "How? What happened?"

Emory put the cap back on the bottle. "They were with the Lieutenant a little ways behind us when that last earthquake hit. It knocked us off our feet, and when it stopped, the section of tunnel behind us was gone. The only thing left was a big mound of rubble fifty feet down. I'm really sorry, Jackson."

Jackson felt numb as he stepped out of the tunnel into the daylight. He moved behind the truck and stared out across the open hills while tears rolled down his cheeks.

Patricia stepped into the sunlight and smiled as she held her arms up and yelled with drunken joy. "Yes! Yes! Yes! I'm freeeee."

The Sargent followed Emory out of the tunnel and saw Jackson standing behind the truck, then she turned to her people. "Let's get back to the base."

Jackson wiped the tears from his cheeks with the back of his hands, then turned around and climbed into the passenger seat of the truck. He hardly noticed the VP and Emory getting into the back seat, then the truck swayed as the soldiers climbed into the truck bed. The driver's door opened, and the Sargent climbed in, but he continued staring straight out the front window as she started the engine and they headed away from the tunnel.

***

THE FACILITY:

Jackson was sitting in the office near the entrance, oblivious to the helicopter landing outside. Sargent Kellerman had sent some of her people into the escape tunnel, and the news was not good. There was no sign of his kids or the Lieutenant, and digging by hand was the only option for recovering the bodies, which would take time to organize and implement.

Sargent Kellerman placed her hand on Jackson's shoulder to get his attention. "Your ride home is here."

Jackson slowly stood up from the chair. "You'll let me know when you recover my children."

"Of course. Again, I'm sorry this happened to you."

"Thanks."

Jackson led the Sargent out of the room and through the security checkpoint, then outside and over to the waiting helicopter, where the rotating blades had cleared the ash from the ground. A soldier wearing a helmet and headset grabbed his hand and helped him up into the helicopter, then showed him where to sit. He looked over at Tremble and Renner sitting in two of the seats, both looking as dejected as he felt.

When the side door shut, he stared out the window as the helicopter climbed into the air. The landscape seemed surrealistic, with the only color that of the brown circle of dirt in front of the entrance to the facility.

Chapter 26

THE RIVER:
The gray snow had stopped falling soon after they left the tunnel, and breathing was easier over the past fifteen minutes as they jogged along the trail back to the dock. They staggered to a stop at the top of the ramp, grateful the skiff was still there. Geneva remained standing while looking at Rhonda, who was bent over while holding her side. "Are you okay?"

"I will be. I'm still out of shape from being on the space station for so long."

"Take your time while I go brush the ash off the windshield."

Rhonda straightened up. "No, let's get going."

Rhonda went down the ramp and over to the skiff, then untied the stern line while Geneva got in and turned on the windshield wipers. Once the engine was idling, she untied the bow line and stepped over the gunnel into the boat.

Geneva turned the skiff around facing down river, then shoved the throttle forward to the stop. With so many branches missing from the canopy, and no falling ash, it was easy to see up ahead for any obstacles or snags in the water.

Rhonda wanted to tell Geneva what else she had learned about the society, but decided to wait until she was with the others. "Why did you come by yourself?"

"We got into a gunfight with pirates coming up the river. Everyone got shot except for me and Brian. That's one of the new passengers. Marcus insisted I keep him below before the shooting started."

"Was anyone killed?"

"Only the bad guys. Marcus was injured the worst. He was shot in the thigh and lost a lot of blood, but he's getting better. Olivia had a bullet go through her right bicep muscle, and Rickie got shot in the ass. Oscar, that's the second passenger, had a bullet go through his left shoulder, but now everyone is recuperating. That's why I came by myself."

"I'm glad you're all still alive. Did Vincent ever show up?"

Geneva looked over at her and smirked. "In a way. You'll see when we get there."

Rhonda noticed the damp ash causing the branches of the canopy to snap or bend across the water. "When did it rain?"

"Just after we left this morning."

"Six hours ago? Wow! It seems like it was ten."

"I know what you mean, with the gunfight and all?"

Geneva slowed the skiff as they approached an obstacle course of heavy limbs. With Rhonda's help, they were able to go under or around them, but it seemed to be taking forever.

When the river widened enough to go fast, Rhonda checked her watch. "Damn! Seventeen minutes to go. I hope the *Windancer* is close."

"According to your map, it should be just up ahead."

Both women stood up to stare over the windshield as the water narrowed around a bend in the river, then hung on as Geneva slowed the skiff. A few moments later, they grinned at each other when they saw the *Windancer* still anchored in the center.

Rhonda recognized the raft on the beach as they approached the port side of the ship. She felt Geneva nudge her elbow while pointing at the shore, then she saw the shoulders and dark head protruding above the sand. She flinched when she heard the skiff's horn blow, then watched a swarm of insects rise into the air above the head. "I see what you mean about Vincent. Did the pirates do that to him?"

"Nope. It was more than a dozen children with spears and a wild pig. I thought it was a fitting way for him to die."

"I suppose it is ironic. I wonder why he didn't come back before we left here yesterday morning."

"I don't care."

Rhonda looked downriver at the pleasure craft anchored close to the far shoreline. It appeared every window was full of bullet holes. "That must have been one hell of a gunfight."

"I know. Too bad I didn't get to help. Grab the bow line and tie us off when I come alongside the ship."

Geneva eased the skiff next to the *Windancer*, then smiled and waved at Olivia stepping out of the pilothouse to raise the section of railing. Rhonda tied the bow rope off to a cleat, then as the skiff swung around into the current, she set the rubber bumpers between the two craft.

Geneva studied Rhonda's knot to be sure it would hold, then shut off the engine and climbed out onto the *Windancer*. "Is everyone still okay?"

Olivia gave her a hug. "Yes, we're all getting better. Rickie is too sore to walk, and I'm having a hard time keeping my dad in his bed, but I'm just glad you made it back safely. I see you picked up a passenger."

Geneva looked over at Rhonda waiting in the skiff. "No, I rescued a friend. I'll explain everything later, because we need to get moving down river in a hurry. We only have a matter of minutes before the volcano erupts."

"You mean you did it?"

"Yeah, we hope so, now start the engines and get ready to bring the anchor up once we have the skiff onboard."

Oscar reached the top of the stairs onto the main deck and smiled at Geneva. "What can I do to help?"

"I'm not sure. Just stand by for a minute while I get the skiff up."

While Rhonda was attaching the slings to the small boat, Geneva heard the low rumble of the *Windancer*'s engines from the stern. She saw the anchor line and remembered the last time they brought it up. "Hey, Oscar. Grab the nozzle of the hose from that reel and get ready to rinse the mud off the anchor chain as Olivia brings it up."

"I understand."

Geneva studied Rhonda's work, then signaled for her to get out of the skiff. She used the winch to hoist the small boat out of the water while Rhonda untied the bow line to guide the craft into the storage bracket, then she turned to the rear window of the pilothouse. "Bring the anchor up and start heading downstream."

While Rhonda was tightening the straps on the skiff, she noticed the insects suddenly leave Vincent's head. Behind him, globs of wet ash fell from the overhead branches, splattering onto the sand. A deep rumble drifted down river from far away, then she looked into the open rear windows of the pilothouse at Olivia. "That must be the heat exchangers. I imagine the magma is rising to the surface, so we need to get out of here fast."

Geneva waited outside the pilothouse, watching Oscar spraying the anchor chain as it was pulled out of the water. When she realized they were not moving, she remembered her lesson and looked through the window at Olivia. "Bring the centerboard up!"

When Olivia pressed the button on the control console, the change was instantaneous as the ship moved forward, nearly knocking Oscar over the stern. The ship quickly gained speed and steerage, racing past the dead bodies on the pleasure boat. Once Oscar joined her at the hose reel, Geneva patted him on the shoulder, then they went inside and she looked over at Olivia. "I'm going down to see grandpa."

When Geneva ran down the stairs, Rhonda moved over next to Olivia, who was steering with one hand. "How are you holding up?"

"I'm fine, but I'm surprised to see you again. What made you change your mind?"

Rhonda watched Oscar and a stranger moving forward between the hatch covers on the main deck. "Did Geneva tell you about the ritual?"

"Yes, but Brian didn't believe it."

"Is that the person with Oscar?"

"Yes, they asked to come with us. They're okay."

"It's true about the ritual, and there's more. They recycle everything, including the people they are killing. Those seamless clothes they wear are made from tanned human skin, and some of them think it's a privilege to eat human flesh."

"Thanks. That helps lessen my feelings of grief and regret for destroying their society."

***

Geneva entered the room and found Marcus staring out through the rear window. "Hey, Grandpa. I think we did it."

Marcus turned his head to smile at his brave granddaughter. "I knew you could." He indicated the rear window. "Did you see that?"

She entered the room and moved across to see what he was talking about, then grinned when she saw a white tower of steam rising into the air. "Is that from the magma?"

"Yes, but above ground it's called lava. It's flash boiling the river water as it moves downhill."

"Will it follow the course of the river?"

"More than likely."

"Then it looks like it's catching up with us."

"You're correct. How does it look down river?"

"I don't know. Once we were underway, I came straight here."

Marcus sat up and placed his good leg over the edge of the bed. "Give me a hand getting up to the pilothouse."

"No, Grandpa. You could open up your wound."

"I need to know what's going on around my ship, so hand me that spear handle Oscar made into a crude crutch for me." When she didn't move, he grabbed his left leg and swung it over the edge of the bed, grimacing in pain, but determined to get up.

Geneva hoped her defiance would make him stay in bed, even after he moved his injured leg over the side. When she saw his anguish, she thought he would stop. He suddenly grabbed the nightstand and pushed his body off the bed, but when he swayed, she ran to his side to grab his waist. Once he was steady, she looked up into his eyes. "You sure are stubborn."

"Are you going to help me or not?"

She grabbed the spear shaft leaning against the wall and placed it in his hand, then held on to his waist as they headed out of the room. When they reached the stairs, she stopped at the bottom and hollered up into the pilothouse. "We could use some help down here."

When Rhonda appeared at the top of the steps, Geneva smiled and eased Marcus into view. "He insists on being in the pilothouse, but it will take both of us to get him there."

Rhonda hurried down the stairs and draped one of Marcus's arms over her shoulders while Geneva did the same with his other arm, then they helped him hop up the steps. When they stepped into the pilothouse, they eased him into one of the captain's chairs next to Olivia.

Marcus studied the river ahead, then opened a drawer below the control console and brought out a paper pad. He flipped to the last entry and found his notes, then searched the riverbanks for the odd formations.

He felt a hand on his shoulder and looked over at Geneva, who was looking at his notepad. "While we were coming upriver, I made notes about the different unusual landmarks or vegetation, adding comments about bends in the river or dangerous areas to avoid on the way back."

Geneva studied his writing where his finger was pointing. "Big ass boulder? Keep to port side coming back? Very descriptive, but why add ass to the size?"

Marcus grinned and pointed his arm downstream. "Do you see that ridgeline about four hundred yards ahead? Keep an eye on it as we get closer."

When the angle changed, Geneva grinned when a massive boulder looked like a giant butt. "Cool."

Rhonda was standing in front of the rear windows, staring at the towering wall of steam and brown smoke from the burning vegetation rising behind them. "You might want to go faster. I think the lava is catching up with us."

Geneva turned around while Olivia and Marcus spun their chairs to the rear of the room. They could only catch glimpses of the steam and smoke through the gaps in the vegetation above their heads, but the leading edge was only a mile behind them.

Marcus turned back to the controls and saw they were already cruising at two-thirds of full speed. He checked his notes and saw when they made the next turn to starboard, they would reach some rapids through a long straight stretch of the river.

He heard Olivia gasp and looked up to see her staring behind them. He spun around, and through a wide gap in the foliage, saw a massive tongue of red lava at least half a mile wide flowing down the side of the mountain.

He spun back around as they approached the bend in the river. Just as he turned into the curve, he shoved the throttles to full power. The momentum forced them to the port side of the rapids, but with the ship being one hundred feet long, they were not tossed around like a raft or kayak.

It only took a few minutes to make it through the churning water, then as the river widened, it slowed down. Marcus tried to determine their speed, but with the constant change in the flow of the water, he could only estimate they were doing twenty-three knots. He checked his notes, then studied the shoreline. "We should reach the entrance soon."

Geneva moved over beside her grandpa. "I wonder if that rope is still across the river."

"I doubt it. The pirates had to cut it to get that boat through."

Rhonda turned from the back window to look at Marcus. "I hope you're right, because that lava is gaining on us really fast."

Marcus glanced back at the towering wall of steam and brown smoke, now less than a quarter mile behind the ship, and gaining fast. When he turned forward, he steered around the next bend in the river and his heart leapt into his throat as he pulled the throttle back to full reverse. The wall of tangled vines and leafs was still stretched across the river, with a gap in the foliage where the pirate's boat had gone through over the top of the rope.

Olivia studied the riverbank where she and Rickie had fastened the rope around the boulder, then at the space where the other boat had gone through. "Can we do like they did and go over the rope?"

"If we try, there's a chance our propeller motors will snag the rope and we'll get stuck."

"Okay, we can use the skiff to get someone to hack through the rope."

Geneva was looking behind them. "There's not enough time. We go now or we're cooked. Maybe the propellers will cut the rope for us."

Marcus grabbed the microphone for the PA system. "You on the bow. We're going to try to go through that wall of vegetation. Get down on the deck and hang on to something."

He waited until his passengers were ready, then shoved the throttles to the stops. The *Windancer* quickly gained speed, heading right for the same spot the pirates had used. The bow slid over the rope and they felt it dragging along the bottom of the ship, then everyone was hurled forward as the ship abruptly stopped.

Marcus tried rotating the rear thrusters to turn the ship at an angle to the rope, hoping one of the propellers would slice through, but it didn't work. "Damn! The rope is caught on the propeller motor housing."

He put the motors into reverse to back away, but the ship only slid sideways along the rope, then he put the motors in neutral and turned to Geneva. "Take a machete and see if the rope is close enough to hack through it."

Rhonda spun around to her friends. "There's no time! Look!"

Everyone stared behind the ship at the distorted glow of the raging lave six hundred feet behind them. A wave of hot air rushed through the open windows, forcing the ship to point forward again, then they watched in numb shock as a massive wave of steaming water rushed downstream ahead of the magma. The *Windancer* was suddenly lifted into the air, turning sideways because of the rope. When it suddenly snapped, the ship straightened out and Marcus shoved the throttles to full ahead.

Even as the ship raced from the river into the ocean, the lava was still flowing faster than the speed of the ship, and would cover them in a matter of minutes. Marcus had an idea and pressed the button on the control console, then watched the main mast rise off the deck, but it appeared to be moving in slow motion. When it finally locked into place, he pressed another button and the main boom dropped perpendicular to the mast, then the sail was pulled up to the top.

Marcus felt the heat on his back through the open rear window as the lava got closer. The main sail suddenly snapped taut, and the ship lunged through the water. He glanced back for a moment and saw he was staying even with the flow, then started the sequence to bring the other two masts up. Moments later, the two sails snapped taught in the wind, and he sighed with relief as they slowly pulled away from the lava.

Geneva wrapped her arms around her grandpa's neck. "Great job!"

Olivia gave Marcus a kiss on the cheek. "Thanks, Dad."

Chapter 27

THE LOWER FACILITY:

The air was thick with dust, dampening the sound of coughing coming from under a massive slab of concrete. A gray-colored hand poked through a gap, shoving loose rock and dirt out of the way. It moved out of sight, then more stone and gravel was shoved to the side. On the fifth push, an arm came through, followed by a head with grayish-red hair.

Hershey could not see a thing in the darkness while she used her free hand to scoop loose dirt and bits of concrete from under her chest. She squeezed her shoulders through, then pushed with her feet and pulled with her hands until her hips and legs slid through the opening.

She spun around and dragged her pack out from under the slab, then retrieved her flashlight and turned it on. She slid the backpack out of the way to kneel over the opening, and aim the light inside. "Clark? Nancy?"

Clark crawled toward the light. "I'm here!"

Hershey moved the beam around the narrow space under the slab. "Nancy? Can you hear me?"

Clark abruptly stopped and turned around on his belly to look further back under the concrete. "Nancy! Answer me!"

Nancy coughed to clear her throat, then turned on her flashlight and aimed it at Clark's face. "You don't have to yell."

Clark raised his hand to block the light in his eyes. "Okay. Are you hurt?"

Nancy lowered the beam of light. "No, but the frame of my backpack is bent and stuck. I think it saved me from being crushed."

"Can you move?"

"Yes, so get out of my way."

Clark turned around on his belly, then continued crawling toward the light. When he reached the opening, he felt Hershey's hand pulling his, as he crawled through. He moved out of the way, then Nancy came through with ease.

Hershey helped Clark get up, then he did the same for his sister. Both ladies aimed the beams of their lights around what was a twenty-foot square room. Rows of shelves were supporting boxes with labels for plumbing fittings, electrical parts, light bulbs, and more they could not see from a distance in the dark.

Hershey's light reflected off a door, then she moved across the room and grabbed the handle. It opened and she stepped through into a large mechanical room, with multiple circuit breaker and control panels. When none of the indicator lights for the controls was on, she began reading the labels.

Clark could see nothing without his own flashlight, which was still in his backpack somewhere under the slab. He moved out of the way for Nancy to enter, then followed her as she moved around the small room. "I wonder if this is part of the main underground facility."

Hershey saw a green button labeled AUX POWER and pushed it. A moment later, the indicator lights came on, as did the overhead lights. She turned off her flashlight and noticed a diagram of the electrical system throughout the underground part of the facility.

Clark moved back to look at where they had fallen through the ceiling. Two light bulbs had not been shattered by the collapse, which allowed him to see the pile of dirt and rock on top of the large slab of concrete with no steel bars sticking out through the sides. "We're not getting out this way."

Hershey sensed Clark and Nancy move up beside her, and pointed to a section of the diagram. "We'll follow this corridor to that intersection, then we can get to the main tunnel up to the surface."

Clark studied the diagram for a moment. "Yeah, but the Sargent said the tunnel to get down here had caved in, and we still won't be able to get out."

Nancy didn't like the idea of staying down there. "Maybe we can dig through from this side?"

Hershey agreed with her. "We have to go see if it's possible."

Clark reached down and grabbed Hershey's backpack. "I'll carry this for you."

Hershey smiled. "Thanks."

Clark slid the pack on to his shoulders and followed the ladies out through one side of the double doors into a short hallway, then through another set of doors into a main corridor. He studied the bare concrete ceiling, noticing fresh fractures, but nothing significant. "This is much better."

When the women went across to a large map of the entire facility, he stopped behind them to look over Nancy's head at the layout of the underground complex. "They weren't joking around. This placed is massive."

Hershey dragged her fingertip across the surface of the map. "We go right along this tunnel to the end, then go left, which will take us to the entrance."

The trio walked side by side with Clark in the middle, occasionally stepping on a few flakes of concrete, but so far, the facility seemed to be intact. When they reached the end, they turned left and followed the curved tunnel. They began seeing larger fractures in the ceiling and walls, then bigger pieces of concrete on the floor.

The damaged continued to get worse for the next sixty feet, then the lights were gone and they could go no further. Large sections of the ceiling had collapsed onto the floor and were buried under a mountain of dirt and rock.

Nancy put her hands on her hips in frustration. "This is just great! It's going to take us years to dig our way out!"

Clark tried to comfort her by placing his hands on her shoulders as he looked into her eye. "I'm sure they'll be digging from the other side with equipment, so it shouldn't take too long."

Nancy shook his hands off her shoulders. "Oh yeah? What about Emory and the VP? If they make it out and rescue dad, they'll tell him we died in a cave in, and they won't be in a hurry to get our bodies. If they don't make it out, it will still take time for dad to be rescued. Who knows how long we'll be stuck down here."

Hershey waited until Nancy calmed down before sharing her thoughts. "First, we need to locate some food and water. According to the map, the mess hall is back the other way from the utility room. Are you ready to get started?"

Nancy did not answer as she spun around and headed back to the other corridor. She heard the footsteps of her companions, then their conversation.

Clark strolled beside Hershey as they followed his sister. "If this place is set up to sustain a bunch of people for a couple of years, we should have no problem living down here for a while."

Hershey looked over at Clark and smiled. "At least the company won't be too bad."

Nancy quickened her pace. "Give me a break!"

***

Six hours later, Clark strolled into the mess hall and found Hershey sitting at a table. "I guess I'm not the only one who couldn't sleep."

"I'm having a hard time wrapping my brain around the idea I might be down here for a while. I just wish I could get word to my husband that I'm still alive."

Clark's jaw dropped for an instant. "Does he live near here?"

"Our house is in Fort Collins, and he's an officer in one of the battalions."

"How did you end up out here?"

"An hour after the asteroid hit Yellowstone, I received orders to come here and open up the facility."

"Do you think Nancy is right about being rescued?"

"I do."

Clark double checked Hershey's ring finger to make sure he was not mistaken, then looked across at her. "When I didn't see a wedding ring, I thought you were single."

She smiled at him. "I'm sorry if I gave you the wrong impression. I was at home when they called. In fact, I had just stepped out of the shower, and in my rush to get started, I accidently left my wedding ring on the nightstand." When she noticed Clark trying to hide his smirk, she grinned at him. "You aren't imagining me naked, are you?"

"What? Oh, no, of course not. Hey, have you seen my sister?"

"Yes. About half an hour ago. Her exact words were, I'm not staying in this hellhole any longer than necessary, then she took off."

"She can be stubborn. I'm going to get better acquainted with what's in the pantry."

"I don't have anything better to do, so I'll join you."

***

Nancy stopped to study the map on the wall at an intersection of four corridors. Her plan was to search every foot of the complex until she either found a way out, or died trying. Now that she had a better feel for how long each corridor actually was compared to the map, she realized it could take months to search all of it.

The map showed the right corridor would take her to the hydroponics station, and she knew it meant there would be running water and air, and there could be some way to get to the surface. Going straight ahead would take her to general housekeeping, but she had a strange feeling she should go down the left corridor, even though the map showed it ended in a storage room.

She turned left, passing three locked doors before reaching a set of double doors at the end. She shoved one side open, then entered a large dark room. She reached around to the wall and flipped a switch, then overhead lights illuminated rows of shelves ten feet high. What surprised her was they were empty.

She strolled along the rows while reading the labels of items not there. It appeared one row was going to be dedicated for artist's paintings, and another to literary classics. When she reached the end, she was about to go down the next row when she noticed something out of place. There was an alcove with a steel door at the back, which had a commercial refrigerator-style handle.

When she stepped into the alcove, something about the size looked familiar. The door was six feet high by eight feet wide, which was unusual for a refrigerator or a freezer. She saw there was a padlock through the handle, and grabbed the base and pulled three times, but it didn't open. She studied the walls for a key, but didn't see one, then went back in to the storage room and searched everywhere for the key.

When she couldn't find it, she took a moment to try to remember where she had seen the door before, then grinned as she burst through both double doors in to the corridor. She jogged to the intersection, then turned right back toward the maintenance storage room.

***

MESS HALL:

Nancy entered the large room, but didn't see Clark or Hershey. They were not in their bedrooms, the recreation area, or anywhere along the way from the mechanical room. She heard voices coming from the pantry and ran inside to find them rummaging through the packaged goods. "I think I found a way out!"

Clark dropped a package on the floor, while Hershey set hers on a shelf as they turned to look at his sister. Clark noticed the bolt cutters in her hands. "Where can you use those?"

"Remember when we first entered the escape tunnel? We passed that big sheet of metal in the wall, and I think I found the other side of it."

"Why bring the bolt cutters?"

She grinned. "You'll see."

Nancy turned and headed out of the pantry, and Clark and Hershey looked at each other before following her in to the mess hall. When they reached the corridor, they were both surprised when they had to jog to keep up.

***

Nancy handed the bolt cutter to Clark. "I don't believe this is a refrigerator."

Clark spread the handles apart while Hershey held the arm of the lock up for a good place to cut the loop. He waited until she let go, then pulled the handles together. When it did not cut it in half, he used all his strength to bring the handles together, then heard the snap as the steel parted.

Nancy grabbed the parts of the lock and tossed them aside, then pulled the handle. Her heart was racing as the latch released, but when she pulled, the door didn't open. She yanked on the handle, grunting with frustration each time, but finally stopped and leaned back against the door.

Hershey had an idea and turned to Clark. "Let me have those cutters. You and Nancy pull on the handle while I beat this against the outer edges of the door and maybe I can break it free."

Hershey waited while Nancy and Clark each placed a hand on the handle. "Okay. Here we go."

Nancy and Clark pulled while ducking out of the way of the swinging bolt cutters. When Hershey became tired and stopped swinging, Nancy let go of the handle, but Clark pushed against the door and it moved a fraction of an inch. He began yanking and pushing while Hershey continued beating. When it stopped coming out, he put his foot against the wall beside the door and pull with all his might.

Hershey was getting tired, but gritted her teeth and swung as hard as she could. The bolt cutters slammed into the top of the door, then the door slammed into her and Nancy, knocking them both to the ground. Clark tumbled backward onto the floor beside them, then all three began laughing when they saw the original escape tunnel on the other side.

***

SPRINGFIELD, MISSOURI:

Jackson thanked the helicopter crew for the ride, then climbed out and hurried to the hangar. He slowly strolled around to the back of the building and pressed the remote button to unlock his ash covered SUV. He started the engine, but did not put the transmission into drive.

He heard a ring tone as the sound system came on, then he looked at the screen and saw he had an incoming call. He touched the green dot on the screen and an unknown caller message appeared, then he touched accept. "Hello?"

"Dad"

He sat in shock for a moment. "Nancy?"

"Yes, Clark and I are safe and out of the facility."

Jackson smiled as tears of joy ran down his cheeks. "You just made me the happiest man in the world."

"We're getting a ride in a helicopter to get home."

"I'll be waiting at the airport."

"Oh, and another thing. Since we've become friends with the Vice President, she is going to set up a surprise for us by the time we get there. I love you, Dad."

"I love you too, and I'll see you soon."

Jackson touched the icon to end the call, then a woman's voice came from the stereo speakers, announcing by some miracle, Yellowstone has settled down, as has the increasing activity along the Pacific Rim. As the announcer continued to explain what would happen next, he leaned back in his seat and smiled.

Chapter 28

CAMP DAVID:

Brill hung up his phone and smiled over at Grant. "We didn't lose any people at the Fort Collins facility." His smile turned into a frown. "I want the Justice Department to launch a full criminal investigation into the contractor who built that underground complex. Hell, have them investigate all the subcontractors, too. I want heads to roll."

Grant smirked at the President. "Yes, Sir."

"Start making arrangements to provide humanitarian aid to all those affected by the ash."

"Yes, Sir. What about other nations?"

"I said to *all* those affected. Do I need to be any clearer?"

"No, Sir. I'll get started right away."

"What about that favor Patricia asked for the Atwaters?"

"The arrangement has already been set in motion."

"Good. Now go get started on the aid packages."

When Grant closed the door behind him, Brill pressed a button on the phone console. "Get me through to Buckingham Palace. Tell them I have some good news to share with the King and Queen."

Chapter 29

WINDANCER

Marcus maneuvered the *Windancer* to the side of the river of lava flowing into the ocean. The roar of hissing steam added to the surrealistic scene as the magma cooled, causing it to build up and spread out from the shoreline in a growing field of new basaltic rock.

Geneva tried getting a station on the radio as they cruised back and forth in an ever widening arch, but the only sound from the speaker was static. She turned it off and studied the giant swath of glowing red lava flowing through the forest, leaving a wall of smoke from the burning jungle.

She suddenly remembered the other radio Rickie had set in a cabinet under the chart table and bent over to bring it out, then got Rhonda's attention. "Show me how to use this thing."

Rhonda moved to Geneva's side as she placed the radio on the chart table. When she turned it on, they heard a man on Earth speaking to a woman on Mars, explaining how their children had almost died during an earthquake, then they heard the voices of two young people talking to their mother.

Geneva looked over at her family. "Who would believe we're listening to someone crying on another planet?" Another thought occurred to her. "Who's going to believe our story?"

Marcus heaved a deep sigh of resignation. "No one. If we tell anyone how we stopped the eruptions, they'll claim we're either crazy or looking for publicity."

Rhonda leaned back against the chart table. "I don't want to end up on the cover of a magazine. I'm just glad to be alive."

No one spoke while they listened to the conversations between people on Earth and those on Mars. They looked at each other, then smiled when they heard how glad the Mars colonists were to learn they would not be the last humans in the solar system.

The end.

Award-winning author James M. Corkill is a Veteran, and retired Federal Firefighter from Washington State, USA. He was an electronic technician and studied mechanical engineering in his spare time before eventually becoming a firefighter for 32-years and retiring. He has since settled into the Smokey Mountains of western North Carolina and has a fantastic view from his writing desk.

He began writing in 1997, and was fortunate to meet a famous horror writer named Hugh B. Cave, who became his mentor. In 2002, he rushed to self-published a dozen copies of Dead Energy so his wife could see his book published before she was taken by cancer. When his soul mate was gone, he stopped writing and began drinking heavily.

His favorite quote. "When you wake up in the morning, you never know where the day will take you."

In 2013, he met a stranger who recognized his name and had enjoyed an old copy of Dead Energy, except for the ending. When she encouraged him to start writing again, he realized this chance meeting was just what he needed to hear at the right moment. He quit drinking and began the rewrite of Dead Energy into The Alex Cave Series, and thankful for that fateful encounter.

You can contact him at:
Jamesmcorkill@gmail.com

Other books by James M. Corkill.

Dead Energy. The Alex Cave Series Book 1.
Cold Energy. The Alex Cave Series Book 2.
Red Energy. The Alex Cave Series Book 3.
Gravity. The Alex Cave Series Book 4.
Pandora's Eyes. The Alex Cave Series Book 5.
DNA. The Alex Cave Series Book 6.
Parallel. Then Alex Cave Series book 7.

Made in the USA
Columbia, SC
25 April 2024

7870272e-8d27-4a2e-a301-45bf1da74369R01